Story
Plot
One

John Gillibrand

 www.trafford.com

North America & international
toll-free: 1 888 232 4444 (USA & Canada)
phone: 250 383 6864 ♦ fax: 812 355 4082

Prologue

ETHEL SAT ON her bed. She dealt her cards from her Tarot pack. Reading her readings and giggling, quietly to herself. She felt a sudden breeze in the room. She looked around, but the doors and windows were still closed.

The curtains rustled in the breeze.

'Help me Ethel, help me. For I seem to be cursed in eternal confusion', she heard a ghastly sigh heave.

'Who are you?', thought Ethel.

'Aah! ... Aah! I`ve found you at last. I can hear your sorrow at being locked up. Help me! Oh help me! For I am now doomed. If I can find you, will you look after me, all of your life?', thought the ghostly sigh, as the curtains rose and fell, in the wind, and the breeze made Ethel feel cool in her room.

'Oh let me see! I'll have to ask my cards. Who do you aspire to be?', asked Ethel, thoughtfully.

The breeze gusted. The ornaments rattled on her bedside table, as Ethel's curtains blew in the wind.

'I cannot remember', came back the reply.

'Then I'll do you a reading, for free', thought Ethel, 'Tell me who you might be? And I'll ask my cards what they see'.

The breeze blew stronger, and then resided a little. 'Ok, agreed! I've been dead for a while, but I can't rest easy', thought the ghostly sigh, as the breeze blew stronger in Ethel's face.

Ethel shuffled her cards. Split the deck of seventy-eight cards. 'I'll draw the first one for you and for truth, to see if I should flee from you', she thought.

She picked up the card, and turned it over.

Death! The thirteenth card.

The breeze blew a gust. All Ethel's ornaments rattled and once again the curtain blew up. 'Oh settle down ghost. It proves you spoke truth, and as such I shall gift you a fresh start', thought Ethel.

The ghost ran amok in the room for a few moments, and then the ghostly voice said, 'Oh Ethel! Oh Ethel it's true, but what of you? Can you help me a lot?', as once again the breeze took up a gust.

Ethel laughed, 'Oh you're so funny. It's got to be true. I'll tell you what, I'll ask my cards what I should do'. Ethel picked up her cards and began to shuffle, as the gust blew into Ethel's face and around the room.

'Oh what should I do for this new friend of mine? Oh where shall I find them? And how shall I help her?', asked Ethel, of her cards, as she once again split her deck of cards and drew one out.

The hanged man! The twelfth card.

The ghostly voice roared in disdain. Ethel shrieked with hysterical laughter for a moment, and then thought, 'Oh fear not you beastly ghost, for it means you only await for my help. I'll do you a deal, with all post-haste. I'll start looking for a way to help you'.

The ghostly voice started to laugh. The breeze sub-sided, then it sounded a sob.

'Now I feel sorry for you. You sound almost in pain, so I'll read you a card of the outcome of years of research', thought Ethel cheekily.

'Would you really do that for me?', thought the ghostly sigh.

'Oh yes, but you might have to guide me, but you can't have my body and I must always have my own way', thought Ethel, with a laugh.

'Agreed, but please, let me live awhile, whilst I'm inside you', said the ghostly sigh.

'I`ll try to decide, but I must ask my cards, for their advice is by how I found you', said Ethel. She felt the breeze rise.

'Oh yes! Oh yes! Oh one more card for me. Anything to get out of eternal misery', thought the ghostly sigh.

'Ah…. let me see! You have others besides you. Who might they be?', thought Ethel, as she picked up her cards and began to shuffle them again.

The breeze blew a gust, 'They are others like I. Trapped in torment and misery, whilst we committed no crime', thought the sigh.

'Together you're united, but what of I? What will become of I, with you lot, inside of me?', thought Ethel.

The ornaments rattled and one tumbled down, but still the gust, blew in Ethel's face, making her smile in pleasure.

'And what is to become of me, if I take on such a quest, to release you from torment and misery in death. Will I ever be free or will I ever marry?', thought Ethel, into the gust of wind, that rattled her room, as she cut her pack of cards, picked up the final card, to reveal:

The lovers. The sixth card.

The room rumbled as the view outside went dark. The wind blew wildly into her face. A picture fell from the wall.

"Agreed", she thought and shouted at the same time.

The Ghosts roared in pain and misery. Ornaments started to fall. She felt the presences, one by one, go inside of her, announcing their intent as they went in.

She heard her mother calling out her name, could hear her running up the stairs, and could hear the laughter and joy, and relief of the first, soon to be the last, inside of her.

Her bedroom door opened. She turned, saw her mother look in awe, around the darkened room, with ornaments still vibrating, until her mother locked eyes with her.

'I'm coming in, I'm the last one in. We will keep our deal. We are bound by it. Please don't give up, and end up like us', thought the ghostly sigh, 'You find us'. Ethel felt a momentary blackening off her memory. The breeze stopped. Ethel smiled at her mother.

"What's going on? What's all the confusion? Why is the picture not on the wall?", asked Ethel's mother. Ethel wanted to smile again.

'Don't tell her', they called from inside of her.

"And who are you?", snapped Ethel, trying to appear calm. Still wanting to smile.

"Oh Ethel! Don't be like that", said Ethel's mother.

"Like what? I'll tidy up later. I'm just playing with my cards", said Ethel.

"I'll speak to the Priest", said Ethel's mother.

'No!', called out Ethel's ghosts from inside of her.

"Not the Priest, but maybe the police", said Ethel, calmly to her mother.

'Good choice!', Ethel's new friends agreed.

"Oh Ethel …… Very well then! But it won`t be the last that you hear about it", said Ethel`s mother. With that, she turned and closed the door behind her.

'He-he-he', thought Ethel and her ghosts, as they started to party inside.

'Now, whose first? I've got my cards. Tell me were it hurts and we'll ask the cards what to do', thought Ethel.

'We're not sure who's first', thought the ghostly sigh.

'Oh! Ok! The one who's been here the longest, why did you die? Why can't you rest? Here …. take hold of the cards. Feel them. Make a wish and shuffle the deck, and I will interpret it for you', thought Ethel.

Chapter one

————•◦•————

"Oh, MOTHER, OH mother, why do you cry?", asked Ethel, of her mother, when she was nine years of age.

"Oh Ethel, please not another rhyme. I can't bear it when you speak to me in rhyme", her mother, Alice replied, "Not now I've been to the police, and they say, they believe you are possessed, but only when you speak in rhyme", she finished, as she held her handkerchief in her right hand, still damp from dabbing her eyes.

"Yes I know. Yes I know. Yes I know, but you have still to say why you cry", continued Ethel, running excitedly from the doorway, into the centre of the room, so she could turn and face Alice. Who, whilst still looking out of the window, had not moved to face her, from when she had spoken in the doorway.

Still no reply.....

"Oh tell me. Oh tell me. Oh tell me, or I shall truly cry", said Ethel, as she started to jump on the spot, looking and sounding both annoyed and irate.

Her mother turned from the window, to look at Ethel, and saw her standing there, in her pink slippers, the blue dress she had recently bought for Ethel, at which, her Ethel had seemed so delighted with, and her own friends hand-me-down blue matching top. "Not now dear. Please wait for an hour or two, until after we've eaten, and I can explain my news, even to you", said Alice with a sigh, as she returned to gazing out of the window.

Ethel fell silent for awhile. She gazed out of the window briefly, but saw only the rose bushes, in their garden, an oak tree rising up in a far off field, and Turner's hill behind. She noticed not the clouds in the sky, whether there were any there or none, if they were white, grey or black, or even if the sun were shining, or if it were night or day.

Then she got an idea, "I know, I know, I know", she continued earnestly, "I'll let you sit a while, and wile away the hours, until my father returns, and you can tell me both together", she said, with a gleeful smile, turned and marched out of the room.

Alice sobbed, 'No, not that', she thought, 'Not now I know the truth, all that kerfuffle over something the police say they can do nothing about. Not here, not in England, maybe in the east, they said, but not here in England, not in this day and age'.

She called out to Ethel, who had left the room, not caring if she was heard or not, "I'll speak to you before then, not only before then, but I'll try to figure out what to say, and how to answer your questions, to both of you, if you have any".

A while later, Alice, stopped sobbing. She went into the kitchen, put her handkerchief in her Laundry drawer, and took some paper tissues back with her, into the sitting room. Once again, taking up her sofa seat and staring out of the window. She thought for a while about what the police had told her, and then began to wonder what to tell Ethel, before her husband returned from work.

"Umm!", pondered Alice, and then she thought, 'How can I explain she is two people, and that I only want one daughter, my daughter, and none of this rhyme, which I thought someone had taught her'. She made to stand, and walk towards the window, but something held her back. 'What`s that?', she suddenly thought.

Then she had the most amazing idea, 'Why not let the stronger one have the body, for it was only the body that she gave birth too'.

She began to ponder the idea, 'How would her husband respond to the rhyme? Surely he wouldn't notice. He's always at work, and what of the baby-sitters? And her family? If worse comes to worse, she could always say she taught Ethel the rhyme. And she could do! Just so she wouldn't have to lie'.

She began to think it through, again and again. The shame of having a well-known possessed child. Why? Well, everybody she knew, knows that it is a sign of bad parenting, but she could conceal it, of course. She smiled in delight at her own idea. No shame. No pain, and possessed or not, the child could make her an awful lot of money..... if she treats it right.

'I can give her what she wants. I know I can. I can make her a whole person. Either one of them. I'm not a bad mother. I know I'm not a bad mother and my husband is not a bad father. This I know to be true', she decided, and then she began to walk towards the stairs, towards Ethel's room. 'Wait!', she thought suddenly, but no, with a strong and firm resolve, Alice moved towards her meeting, with her devil's child.

Just then, the doorbell rang. 'Phew!', thought the house, as Alice froze, then turned, and went to answer the door, only to find it was one of the women from the local leisure committee.

"Hello Alice", said Mildred. "Eric asked me to drop off this here bread for you".

"Oh! Hello Mildred. I wasn't expecting anybody to call", said Alice, quite startled.

"Yes I know", continued Mildred. "Eric said you might be busy about the house, at this time of day".

"Yes, yes, please do come in. I'll put the kettle on for you, if you'd like a cup of tea", said Alice, gesturing Mildred into the hallway and the room beyond.

"Oh thank you! That would be nice. I've always wanted to visit your home", replied Mildred, stepping into the hallway and following Alice into the kitchen, "Where shall I place your bread?", asked Mildred, once inside the kitchen.

"Oh please", said Alice, "Let me take the bread for you", taking the bread and then once again gesturing, but to a chair this time. "And please take a seat, while I put the kettle on the stove". With this, Alice set about lighting the stove and putting the bread into the cupboards, whilst producing cups, tea, and a teapot, from off the shelves, within the kitchen.

"You look like you have had bad news. Why is that? If you don't mind me asking, that is", continued Mildred.

"Well, I have and I haven't", responded Alice, "What draws you to this conclusion? If I may ask".

"Oh, nothing really. Its that your eyes look red and puffy", continued Mildred.

"So?", said Alice, suddenly startled.

"Well, my mother's eyes would look like that, when she received bad news, from time to time. I remember those times occasionally, when I see other people's eyes look the same, that's all! I hope I don't intrude or seem rude to you", finished Mildred.

"No", said Alice slowly, then she turned to the stove and then continued, "I was just in the middle of doing some housework. It was a little dusty, that's all".

"Oh", said Mildred, in surprise, then added, "I never let the dust get too much, not unless I've been away for a few days".

"Yes I know, I mean...... I don't know that, about you, I mean, but I've been feeling under the weather recently, and I've let the housework accumulate a little too much", said Alice.

"Oh", said Mildred. "I don't like the sound of that", she fell silent as the kettle boiled and Alice poured the tea, produced the cups, saucers, tea-pot and sugar bowl, and then a little jug of milk, which she sat down towards the centre of the table.

"Tell me about your day today, and Eric, ... what did he say?", asked Alice. "While I pour the tea for us both, if that is OK".

"Oh, please, let it brew a while", said Mildred. "Your husband is fine. He's busy at work, He asked me to bring it, because it was a gift and he didn't want to forget the bread, on his way home".

"A gift, who from?", asked Alice.

"Oh I can't say, you'll have to ask him yourself, but he knew I was passing by, and asked if I would drop it in", said Mildred. "But you dear, you mustn't feel run-down".

"Yes….. but", said Alice.

"Oh I know, I know, or I think I do, but please pour the tea, if you like. We don't want it going cold now, do we?", continued Mildred.

With that, Alice poured the tea, and added sugar appropriately, and then took a sip of her tea. She then asked Mildred, "Tell me Mildred, what do you think you know?".

Mildred smiled wistfully and then looked out the window "Ah…..", she replied, "I would like to say, but …..", then she also took a sip of tea, smiled again, turning from the window and leaning towards Alice, "I'm a little worried, I might upset your husbands plans, for you and the little one".

Alice froze for an instant, 'Relax', she thought, and let out a slow and gentle sigh. She smiled brightly, "Yes, you're quite right. I don't want to upset my husband, or my child either, for that matter", said Alice, who then turned to look out the same window, suddenly recalling what she was about to do. She glanced quickly at Mildred, who was still sipping her tea, then looked at her own cup, and took another sip herself.

"I like to walk around the village, around the town. Meet people and chat to them", said Mildred, changing the topic of conversation.

"Yes", said Alice, "So do I, from time to time".

"I suppose it must be more difficult for you. Not knowing so many people. Having a child in tow", continued Mildred.

"Yes, I suppose so", said Alice. "I've never really considered the idea".

"What of your child? Does she know many people, old or young in the area?", asked Mildred.

"None, that I'm aware off. I'm thinking of teaching her rhyme though", continued Alice.

"Oh well, if you take her with you, you might find people who can help you", said Mildred.

"Eh?", said Alice.

"With the erm….., rhyming. I don't know many people that rhyme, but then, I don't know all the people around here either", said Mildred, then she continued, "It'll be OK for you, if you're with her. The old folks like people to chat too, and they're generally in their gardens in the summer".

"I hadn't thought of that", admitted Alice.

"She might even meet some friends of her own age or friends for the future, if they're old folks. Even the men are OK around here. It's not like we're city folk", finished Mildred, with a shake of her head.

They chatted a little longer, finished their tea. Alice thanked Mildred again for the bread, and Mildred left to go where she was going, before she stopped by. Alice went back to the sofa, for a rethink, and sat down. Once again looking out of the window, at Turner's Hill. 'An obstacle to overcome', she thought, some what bemusedly.

After a while, she came up with a plan. She left the sitting room and went upstairs. She knocked on Ethel's door but there was no reply, so she casually entered, only to find Ethel, lying face down on the bed, sobbing.

"Ethel dear", said Alice gently, approaching ever so slowly. Ethel looked up at her, tears and tear stains on her face and cheeks, "Please don't cry", continued her mother. She sat down beside Ethel, on the edge of the bed, looked fleetingly out of the window and said, "I want to tell you why I was was crying earlier".

This grabbed Ethel's attention. She quickly got up onto her hands and knees, in the centre of the bed and looked Alice squarely in the eyes.

"But I don't want you to tell anybody", continued Alice. "Can you promise me that?", she asked soothingly.

"Yes, yes, yes I can", said Ethel excitedly. "Tell me, tell me, tell me quickly, quickly, quickly!", she continued, starting to bounce gently on the bed, and mockingly smiling and faking hand-clapping.

Alice let out a long sigh. Felt and sensed a darkening all around the room, and became aware of feeling colder, "Please", she said slowly, "Tell me, without rhyme if you can. I promise not to tell anyone what you are about to tell me".

"No! No! You first, you first. I can't promise, there'll be no tomorrow", said Ethel quickly. Suddenly she sat boldly still, but continued to stare straight into Alice's eyes.

"Please, not you first, but the other Ethel. My Ethel. My baby Ethel who's unpossessed. Can she still speak?", asked Alice.

"Yes", replied Ethel.

"Then her first. Please let her speak", continued Alice.

"Ok, but be quick, be fast and be fair", rhymed back Ethel, as her head fell, to face the floor.

"Ok, my Ethel", said Alice gently, as Ethel slowly raised her head to look at her. "Would you like mother to tell you why I cried earlier?", asked Alice.

"Yes please", said Ethel.

"Can you promise me, not to tell anybody, if I tell you?", asked Alice.

"Yes I will", said Ethel.

"Promise what?", asked Alice beguilingly.

"I promise not to tell anybody what you are about to tell me", said Ethel.

"Ok, then we have a deal. I'll tell you when I've finished, what I've got to say", said Alice.

"Ok", said Ethel.

"Ethel dear?", said Alice.

"What is it?", questioned Ethel.

"Not you. You are my Ethel. I want to speak to Ethel dear. The rhyming Ethel", said Alice.

"Please don't bring her back. Not now I'm free of her", said Ethel.

"Oh, Ethel, she'll only comeback unannounced and you'll only be upset and distraught. I'll make you a deal. You can body share for a while, until I find you or your ghost a body or host, of their own. Please, so I can tell you why I cried, let me speak to the other Ethel, so neither of you can tell, why mother cried". She paused for a moment, drew no response from Ethel, and then continued, "I'll take you around the town, or the village. Anything, or one thing that you like, I will get it for you. No matter how long it may take, and I'll clear your body, down to just one mind. I promise, just one mind", said Alice.

"But.....", said Ethel, trying in vain to comprehend the full meaning of the content.

"I'll introduce you to all the people nearby. I'll find you a gift. It's the only way to clear your mind". Ethel didn't look impressed, but Alice pushed on, full of new resolve, "You may not be able to have all of your will just yet, but you will one day, given time. Your own body too. To do with as you will. Just like you used to, when you were small. You'd like that, wouldn't you?".

Ethel looked suddenly very confused, "But ....", she started but then lapsed into silence.

"But what dear?", asked Alice. "Are you saying you would not want to have your own mind and body?".

"No", said Ethel.

"Then what?", demanded Alice, almost petulantly.

"It's just that I want my mind and body now", said Ethel. "Not tomorrow or the day after. Why can't I have my body and mind now? Please, tell me", finished Ethel.

"I will tell you, but it's why I was crying, you see? Please, you must agree. I must be allowed to speak to the other Ethel, so if she finds out why I cried, she can't tell anybody either. Wherever she might be or whoever she might be. It's the only way I can help you now, because I know you will be with the other Ethel when I go", continued Alice.

"But I don't want her with me any longer", said Ethel.

"Yes, I know, Ethel, but that is why I have to speak to her. It's for your own good, and your own protection, not just for now, but in the long run as well", said Alice, slowly, but firmly.

"Alright, alright, alright", said Ethel quickly, "I will, I will, I will", she continued, before sinking back onto the bed.

"Not you, my dear Ethel, by my Ethel has to let you through", said Alice soothingly.

"No", snapped Ethel, suddenly drawing away from her mother. "Not like that. Not until you tell me, Ethel. Your Ethel. What is going on?", she said, more agitatedly, now.

"I can't dear", said Alice sadly. "Not now you know so much, but won't let me speak to your ghost in rhyme, and then I will release you from the promise you have just made to me".

"I can't do that", said Ethel, "I made a promise not to tell anyone".

"Who too?", asked Alice sternly, "Tell me, who is stopping you from allowing the ghost through?".

"You are, you are, you made me tell. Already I'm trapped and already I know. You must make her sin. You must make her sin, and then I'll be all that you desire", said Ethel quickly, and with a smile.

"Ok", said Alice, "It's your game now. I'll keep your Ethel, to your word, or your promise, and you must choose a gift that you want from somebody, and you must help us to make the person gift it up to you, whether they want to or not, and when they do, either you or your ghost, will have to live in that person's body, but remember, because you promised not to tell anybody, that, because I have started, and haven't finished yet, you can't tell anybody what I have said, especially about why I cried, but also, because you will not let your ghost through to speak to me, and to make the same promise. I cannot tell you why I cried, until either of you live permanently inside somebody elses body".

Ethel just stared at her mother, who got up angrily and left the room.

When Eric came home, Alice called up the stairs, for Ethel to come down for her meal. As Ethel ran downstairs to greet her father, she started to speak, "Hello father! Hello, you'll never guess what's happened today", she said.

"Oh really?", said Eric, with a broad smile, "And what's happened today then? Can you tell me?".

"Yes, yes", said Ethel, "Mother had.....".

"Stop that child", scolded Alice, instantly and abruptly.

"But......", continued Ethel.

"She's been naughty", interupted Alice. "She's not to speak about today. She promised me", she continued.

"But she's only a child Alice. Please let me speak to her. I am her father you know. I do have a right to know. You do know that?", said Eric.

"Not any longer. She made me a promise. She'll do as I say now. You wait and see", said Alice.

Eric looked surprised, then said, "Oh really? Let's see then. Ethel dearest, can you tell me what promise you told your mother? That you made her today?", he asked, quite concernedly.

"I can't say", said Ethel, looking around the hallway, "But maybe I said I would do as she says".

"Why would you make a promise to your mother and not to me? Or both of us?", asked Eric.

"She's promised me a gift and......", continued Ethel.

"Hush child", interupted Alice. "You're to say no more".

"Ethel, please tell me. I am your father. You can trust me to help you. You do know I love you very much as my daughter, even if you've done something wrong or not? I will help you. You do understand that, don't you?", continued Eric.

"Yes, but......", continued Ethel, who then looked towards Alice for guidance.

"Oh leave her be, Eric. She's given her word now. She doesn't want to break her promise, anymore than she wants you to break any of your promises, or your words", said Alice sternly.

"Oh well, if that's the case Ethel. If that's all I'm worth to you. Despite going out, earning the wages to give us our home and that puts tea in our pot, and food on your table, that a gift from your mother, is worth keeping your father out of your life, then I'll do as she asks and keep out of your life from now on", said Eric firmly. "It's up to you. You can make the decision on your own. Whether you want to trust your father or not, or to start keeping secrets from me, and conspiring with others, behind my back, whilst I do my best for you and your mother".

There was silence for a while. Eric broke the silence eventually, "Anytime you want to bring me back into your life, you can do so, but until then, I'll do my best for you both as you know. All you have to do, is tell me, what is so important that you cannot tell your own father? Who, with the aid of mother nature, your mother and the wonders of the world, helped to create you".

"Oh Eric! You don't have to sound so dramatic", said Alice.

"I'll not be cut out of my nine year old daughter's life, treat her as my own, be asked to explain why she does things, the way she does, and then have to admit that I stopped knowing her as a person at nine years of age. You have killed this child to me. I want an explanation, either from you or her, as to what is going on. Until that time, I'll treat her as a foster child, for I'll no be calling her a bastard, because I know she was born into wedlock, as do you. That I know Alice", said Eric.

"Oh Eric, please calm down", said Alice.

"I want to know, either of you can tell me, that's Ethel, or you Alice, as well, and if you have to bring in an outsider to tell me, no matter what has been going on, you'll have to clarify every word of truth to me, that this outsider or outsiders tell me. Am I making myself clear to you both?", continued Eric.

"Yes", they both admitted.

"Ok, then I'm the bread winner in this house now. I can see it's two against one. From now on I'll have to be a little careful around the both of you, but always remember, I'll protect you both from harm, but if you turn on me, in any way, manner or form, I'll turf you both out of my home. It's me who pays the rent. It's me who has his name on the house deeds", said Eric.

"Oh it won't be like that Eric", said Alice, "But we will remember your words on the matter, won't we Ethel?".

"Yes", agreed Ethel.

"Right", said Eric, "I'm going to wash. I'll be back in a few minutes for our dinner". With that, Eric went out of the hall and started to wash.

Alice walked over to Ethel and said quietly, "You my young lady, to keep your promise, and our deal, you are going to have to remember, you can not speak to people freely, any longer. Not until we free your body to one mind".

"Ok", responded Ethel, "I will try harder".

"Good! Is that a promise from both of you?", asked Alice.

"Yes", said Ethel, "I want to be well".

"And you?", asked Alice.

"Yes, yes, but please don't let him go to the police", said Ethel.

"Ok, I won't, but no tricks around your father, and one day you may be grateful that he has always promised to protect you", said Alice.

"Ok, Ok", said Ethel, who then began to skip into the dining room, ready to eat.

Chapter two

————•◆•————

THE NEXT DAY, Eric set out to work early, before Ethel had arisen. When she came downstairs for breakfast, she once again was faced by a solemn looking Alice.

"Where's father?", asked Ethel.

"Oh child, don't start. He's gone to work early. There's an emergency down at the mill, apparently", said Alice, then less harshly, when she saw Ethel's face drop, "But, I'll tell you what, I'll do some breakfast, and then, if it's nice this afternoon, I'll take you for a walk, to see what we can see in the village, and maybe tomorrow we will visit the town closeby", she finished.

"Which town? Which town? Which town closeby? Oh tell me, oh tell me, I don't want to go too far", said Ethel excitedly, jumping up and down, feigning hand-clapping again.

Alice smiled and half-laughed at this. "Oh dear Ethel, why so scared? We have to see our village first", she said soothingly.

Ethel stopped jumping up and down, and smiled. "Yes, you are right", she said; quite precociously, then added, "Tomorrow may never arrive".

"Why don't you like town, all of a sudden?", asked Alice, chidingly, and with a faint smile.

"Well I do, really, but that is where the school is, and I don't want to think about school, until the summer is over", reported Ethel.

"Ok, Ok", said Alice. "We will go around the village and get to know some people, if we can. Maybe even call in on Mildred".

"Mildred?", interupted Ethel, sharply. "Who is Mildred? If I may ask?".

"Oh, I don't think you have spoken to her, or been introduced to her, but she knows your father and seems quite pleasant", said Alice.

"Does she now?", said Ethel, looking thoughtful. "In that case, it had better be nice all day. I like meeting new people now. Especially if they live closeby".

They ate breakfast together and drank some tea. Alice made a shopping list of items that she could buy from the shop close to the mill. They both agreed, what with the emergency at the mill, not to call on Eric, as he would probably be to busy, to see them, and might get into trouble with the owner, if he was still very busy when they went by.

They went their seperate ways for the morning. Ethel playing in the garden with some dolls and Alice did some housework. They both changed their garments, to their best clothes, and then after lunch, set out for a walk around the village, hand in hand.

They came out of their gate, and turned left, towards the village. They passed farmer Guild's wheat field and approached Moira and Philip knight's cottage. Both were in the garden, pruning some of their bushes, with gardening tools, close towards one of their vegetable patches.

"Good morning to you both", said Alice.

"Eh!", said Philip, looking up from his pruning, "And who might you be then?", he asked suspiciously.

"I'm Alice from the next cottage along, and this is my daughter Ethel, who I'm introducing to the village", responded Alice pertly.

"Oh Philip! Do calm down. Hello my dear", said his wife. "I'm Moira. We're pleased to meet you, aren't we dear?", she asked Philip sternly.

"Oh aye! That we are", responded Philip. "Please forgive me if I appeared rude. I've been quite busy today and I haven't had any lunch yet", he said, half closing one eye and looking from Alice to Moira.

"I'm pleased to meet you both", continued Alice, unpreturbed.

"Yes, me too", said Moira. "And how old is the little one then?".

"Oh, she's nine years old", said Alice.

"Does she have a job yet?", asked Philip quite quickly.

"Not yet", responded Alice. "She's still at school".

"Oh aye! That be right", continued Philip.

"Oh do ignore him dear", said Moira, interupting Philip, but not breaking his momentum.

"There'll be plenty of jobs for her down at farmer Guild's farm. I'll bet!", he finished with a smile.

"Oh", said Alice, then continued, "I.....", before being interupted by Moira.

"Oh don't mind him, Philip that is, he don't like to see idle hands, that's all", said Moira.

"Oh, Ok, I'll do my best not to mind his words", finished Alice.

Philip let out a roar of laughter, at this, and said, "Aye, I'll bet ye will".

Moira chuckled and said, "Please excuse my husband dear. He's been out in the sun too long. I'd better take him inside, give him some food, and see if I've any ice or cold water to put onto his head. Good-bye my dear, and your child too. I hope you both have a pleasant day". Without waiting for a reply she went over to Philip and began to lead him inside.

"Good-bye", said Alice, then to Ethel, "Say Good-bye dear. Don't be shy".

"Good-bye, good-bye, to both of you", called out Ethel.

As the couple reached the door of their cottage, Moira turned and waved to Ethel, as Philip said, "Be sure you get to the farm quick, young lady. You might get a job in the shop". At that, Philip and Moira disappeared into their one storey cottage, closing the door behind them.

"What a nice couple", said Alice to Ethel, "And such useful advice". Ethel just stared at her mother. "Come along", she continued, "There's so many people to meet, and the afternoon has only started".

With that, they both continued along the road, crossing the bridge over the river Greendale, passing two more cottages, where there were no signs of life, before taking the right turn, onto the road leading to the mill.

On their left-hand side, just ahead, they saw another cottage.

'Ethel, help me! I'm trapped inside the cottage, and on the mountain', came a ghostly call.

'Why do you call out to me? What about your owner? And how can I help you?', thought Ethel.

'He never speaks to me anymore. He's forgotten who I am. Please keep me company, when you can', came back the answer.

'Oh yes, oh yes, that's another one. We must get the remains', thought a ghostly sigh, 'We can check the cards later, to get a plan, but let's investigate for now'.

Ethel agreed and said quite excitedly, "Oh look, oh look, can we stop for another chat?", to Alice, as Ethel pulled on her arm in excitement.

"Oh alright dear Ethel, but you must promise me you'll be well-behaved, and to speak only when you are spoken too, or

I will pack you off to work on the farm, as Philip asked", said Alice, suddenly feeling a jolt.

The sun suddenly became covered by a cloud, and a cool breeze rose up, leaving Alice, with a shiver and a few goose bumps, for a moment or two.

"Alright, alright, I'll do as you want, but remember you asked me, not to work at the farm", smiled Ethel, quite quirkily and excitedly.

"Alright", said Alice. "I'll play your game, but remember you asked me, to remember, you are not to work at the farm". Alice felt a few spots of rain, unexpectedly. As she looked up to the sky, she saw a few grey clouds, that she had not noticed before.

As they approached the cottage, Ethel heard, 'Come to me Ethel! Come to me… keep me company for a while. I've heard no tales for weeks or months, and I can tell you many a tale', from the ghostly caller.

Ethel tried to run ahead, but Alice restrained her, by asking her to behave. She could make out the man now, seemingly busy, digging or pruning some plants by himself.

"Goodday to you sir", called out Alice, as she and Ethel approached his gate.

"Goodday to you both, and a good afternoon as well, I would, when the sun reappears from behind it's new cloud", replied the man.

"And what does that mean? If I may be bold enough to ask", responded Alice.

"Ah, just a mere jest, for the sun is covered by a cloud". replied the man.

"Is that truly the case?", requested Alice, "Or do you play some trick upon me?", she continued.

"I bid thee that I speak the truth, and I bid thee to speak thy business here, for I have much to do", responded the man.

Alice stood upright, in a dignified horror, for an instant, before continuing, "My name is Alice, and this is my daughter Ethel. She is nine years old".

"I'm very pleased to meet you both, of that I'm sure. What can I do for you both, please? For my time runs short, and I have much to do", said the man.

"I promised my daughter, to introduce her to some of the local villagers, for we are new to the area, and I am hoping to find some people to teach her to rhyme properly", said Alice.

"Oh", said the man, heaving a heavy sigh, "Is that all! Well, I'm very pleased to meet you Ethel, but I know no rhyme. You will have to look elsewhere".

At that, they all heard the sound of approaching horse's hooves, "Who can that be?", asked Alice of the man.

"I'm not too sure", replied the man. "A few of the gentry have horses around here, if you take my meaning?".

"Yes, I do now", said Alice.

Alice and Graeme turned to watch the approaching rider.

'Are you sure he doesn't speak to you?', thought Ethel to the ghost, 'He does seem quite nice and pleasant'.

'He used too but he grows old and wreary. Come inside and I'll tell you of my past', the ghostly caller beckoned.

'Why don't you rest easy? Just so I know. Just in case I'm not allowed in', thought Ethel.

'I'm not a free person. It's written into the Magna Carta, the constitution of the country you're in', thought the ghostly caller. 'Help me Ethel. Help me. Let me rest easy. Don't let the Lords and Masters rule over me eternally. Take my remains, and take them...... Aaaargh', screamed the ghostly caller.

The rider drew level with them. He wore a red peaked cap, red jacket, with black pants and he held a whip between his hands, which both also gently held the reins of the black horse.

He stopped and said, "I say..... and who might you three be then?", authoritively.

"I be Graeme Daniels, and this be my cottage, my Lord", replied the man earnestly.

"Then I'll bid thee, Graeme Daniels, to stay off Heart's Hill and stay closer to your home, least there be trouble from the witches, if you take my meaning?", replied the Lord.

"I only go there for a walk, now and then", said Graeme.

"Yes I know. I have had complaints passed onto me, that you have been seen by the stone circles", continued the Lord.

"Do you mean the ancient burial mound up on the west side of the hill?", asked Graeme with a gulp.

"Aye, I do as that. There's folks around here, no more believe that the stone circle is a burial ground of old, than they believe you, yourself, have been, and still are, by the way, practicing witchcraft from up there. And they will, so they say, do it onto you, if they believe for an instant that it's true", continued the Lord. "So consider yourself well warned in advance. For that is the popular opinion hereabouts, and in the local town of Daleville".

"Thank you my Lord", said Graeme.

At this, Ethel asked, "Where's Heart's Hill?".

"Hush child", said Alice quickly.

The Lord turned onto Ethel with a glare, "You child. You should learn not to interupt. A few years of working the fields at Guild's farm, should turn you away from wanting to learn of witchcraft and curses", he concluded.

"Oh please my Lord! We are new to the area. Please do not take her out of school, so soon", begged Alice.

"Aye, well….. we'll see about that then, but you woman, you need to control your child better and stay out of others affairs. Stay in your home more often and do your husband's bidding, and be a better wife to him, than you are a mother to your child. For now at leastways. Until I say otherwise and I'll decide what to do about your child, dependent upon your husband's performance at the mill.

"My mill, by the way, just so you know. On my land as well, just so you know. As is your home and future, just so you know", said the Lord.

With that, he turned his horse back from the direction from whence he came, and said, "Not another word from all three of thee about this to anyone, or to me, but I'll bid thee all goodday and be off".

At that, he dug his heels into both sides of his horse, clucked a few sounds and galloped off.

"That be Lord Turner, if I'm not mistaken. Is that correct?", asked Alice.

"Aye, that be him, Miss Alice", said Graeme.

"Oh please", said Alice, sounding exasperated, "Call me Alice and allow me to call you Graeme".

"Aye, if you like, Alice", said Graeme.

"What am I to do Graeme?", asked Alice, "I'm new to the area. You heard his Lordship, there is only you I can talk to about this, and I don't know the local customs yet".

"Please Alice or Miss Alice, if you choose. You heard his Lordship. Not another word to anyone about this", said Graeme.

"Oh please Graeme, hear me out. He said from all of us, to anyone else, but not from us to each other", said Alice.

"That's not my understanding of it", said Graeme.

"That's as maybe, but that's not what he said, and you'll no be calling him and I a liar now, will you? Not with witches on your tail, for going to forbidden places. Possibly even at the wrong time of year", continued Alice.

"What know thee of witches, young lady? If I may be so bold as to ask?", said Graeme.

"I'll tell thee over a cup of tea, if you've given time to tell me, a little of your local customs", bartered Alice, and then pushed, "Unless you, like me, want to face your future alone? In uncertainty".

"Why not here, on the road?", asked Graeme.

'Ethel, Ethel, come to me, please', thought the ghostly caller.

"Ooh", said Alice, sounding shocked, "And walls have ears, but birds carry news. What if ought finds out and takes offence, or tells your Lord or Master?".

"It's a good thing you're married, but will your child keep the news safe? Or else we might as well tell our news on the village green, during the next celebration of the full moon", said Graeme.

"Oh aye", said Alice, "She's good at keeping secrets. She made made me a promise. See?", she concluded.

"Ah, that'll be why there's no need for her at the mill then. You'd better come in. It sounds like a fair trade. News for news, but no funny business, or ought like that. Just what we agreed to talk about", said Graeme.

"Agreed", said Alice, and then she said to Ethel, "Can you agree as well Ethel? Not a word about what we talk about to anyone. Not even to the Lord or your father. It will keep you and us (she glanced towards Graeme) out of trouble and off the farm. No matter what anyone says or does".

"Agreed", said Ethel, enthusiastically.

"Are you sure, my dear Ethel?", asked Alice.

"Yes, yes, I'm sure", said Ethel, less enthusiastically than before.

"Then we have a deal?", asked Alice of Graeme.

"Agreed", said Graeme. With that, he began to lead them into his home.

'I'm coming in ghostly caller. Wherever you are. Whoever you are', thought Ethel, as she was led to the back of the cottage.

'Oh Ethel, oh Ethel, I'm trapped inside a container. It's round and it's small, and no-one speaks to me, anymore', thought the ghostly caller.

Graeme led them into his kitchen, proffered seats to them with a gesture, and began to make a pot of tea. Ethel thought, 'I'm inside the kitchen. There's a lot to see. Can you still hear me?'.

Alice and Ethel sat next to each other at the table, proffered by Graeme. "Do you live alone, Graeme?", asked Alice conversationally.

Graeme looked towards the seated pair. "Oh aye", he responded wistfully. "I were married once, but she passed away, through ill-health, shortly after we married", he concluded.

"Oh, I'm terribly sorry to hear that. Did she come from closeby?", asked Alice again.

"Aye!", said Graeme. "I prefer not to talk about it, but she came from Thorberry village, the other side of Isop Hill. From Lord Petersberry's distrcit, if you get my drift?".

"I'm sorry to have to ask, least ye not be liking to speak of it, but did thee, as in the two of you, ever have a problem with witchcraft in the area? Or on the other side of the hill?", asked Alice.

"It's not like that, see? For my parents are passed away. I met my wife whilst over there on duties, for the Post Office, see? For I were younger then, and would travel more freely", said Graeme, then he continued, "Truth of the matter is, both I, my wife, and her family, are not much liked hereabouts, nor the jobs we do, so we have troubles with lots of folks, see?".

"What's not to like of a postman?", asked Ethel quickly, forcing a half-smile from Graeme, but then she looked apologetically at Alice, who continued,

"Hush child. Try not to pay heed to what is said. Least you get us three into trouble one day, with something that is said".

"Aye", sighed Graeme, then he said, "She might as well know. Some folks say, 'No news is good news', and some say, 'Here is the bringer of Bad News', or, 'Here is the bearer of ill-omen', whilst some just glower or say, 'Don't bring that here. I can't even read'".

He looked down, saddened, just as the kettle began to boil. Then he began to pour water into the teapot.

'Ethel....', began the ghosty caller.

'I'm here', thought Ethel quickly, 'But think quick. Guide me too you, and I'll speak only to you', she finished.

Graeme brought the tea to the table on a tray, with cups and saucers, mainly white but with a light blue design on them. He placed the tray down, onto the table. Ethel took the opportunity to look around the room, only to find her eyes were drawn towards a golden egg ornament, sat on the top shelf, of the kitchen shelving.

'Is that you? In the egg? Answer me only if it's true', thought Ethel quickly.

'It's me! It's me! Oh please release me. I feel so trapped, I need some freedom', thought the ghostly caller.

'I'll see what I can do', thought Ethel determinedly.

"Some folks still see postmen as birds of ill-omen, and not just in these parts, if you take my meaning?", finished Graeme.

"Yes, I do", said Alice, sounding very concerned, "That's why I'll help you, if I can. For I don't like to think of men, or even one man, for that matter, being forced to live alone".

"Aye, well, I'll thank ye for that but it's your advice and knowledge I'll be after, on or about witches or witchcraft, but not interference into how I live or whom I choose to live with. If anybody at the moment. If you take my meaning?", said Graeme earnestly.

At that, Ethel jumped up, out of her chair, shouting, "Oh look! Oh look! A golden egg, up by the roof. I want, I want. I want to share your golden egg".

"Oh my!", exclaimed Graeme in surprise. "It was a wedding gift from my ex-wife's family. I can no be giving away a gift of such sentimental value. Not only to me, but to her relatives too".

"Calm down", interjected Alice to Ethel, urgently. "Remember you are not to say. Not only that you were here, but what you saw here, and what you heard here. So as not to give Graeme and I away to the Lord and Master of this area around here".

Ethel fell silent. Her head dropped and she returned slowly and quietly to her seat. "Please accept my apologies, on Ethel's behalf, for her little outburst, for I fear that meeting Lord Turner has given her a shock or two, more than I expected. She is normally much better behaved than this", said Alice to Graeme.

Greame heaved in a deep breath and sighed, "Considering her age and the threat of her work, and accepting that no harm is or was done, then I'll accept your apology on behalf of your daughter Ethel, for creating such a stir, whilst she only came in for some tea, out of the warm".

"Aye, thank thee for that, if I may call thee Graeme", said Alice with glee.

Graeme chuckled again and said, "Aye, I reckon you can Alice. Here! Allow me to pour the tea". Alice nodded in acquiescence, and Graeme poured out three cups of tea. One for each of them, before adding, "Please help yourself to milk and sugar".

Alice nodded her thanks, then poured out the milk for Ethel and herself, added some sugar for them both, stirred the tea and then said, "If its witches that be after thee, always be wary of people in threes. Never accept a blessing or a curse from these, and always be careful to lock your doors. Whether you be, in or out, in the village or in your garden. In your kitchen or fast asleep, for they'll be looking for small items, clothes, or jewelery, hair or finger nails, waste or goods as of yet, not thrown away, so they can cast a spell on you from afar.

"Every time you wonder where that item might be. That's why you can't let them sneak into your home, whether you are home or alone, or out in the road, or climbing mountains and hills, and far out of sight", finished Alice, as she blew on her tea and took her first sip.

Graeme looked at his tea thoughtfully. Seemed to be about to speak, but then raised his tea cup and took his first sip, from his cup.

Ethel gave Alice a nudge. Alice looked at Ethel, who also appeared as if she wanted to speak, but Alice shook her head from side to side, then raised one finger before her lips, then shook her head from side to side more quickly and then gave Ethel a frown.

Ethel looked at her tea cup, sorrowfully, then back to Alice, who was still watching her, and then pointed at the golden egg. She then smiled broadly at Alice, once she realised Alice had seen and caught sight of the golden egg again.

Alice gulped, and then looked back at Graeme, who still appeared to be sipping his tea. Then he surprised her. "I'll tell thee what! If ye like, Alice or Miss Alice to me", he said suddenly, "Maybe it will help to calm Ethel, after her fear, if that be right, if, with your permission of course, I allow her to see my gold plated egg. If she likes to see, that is?".

This time it was Alice who had to stifle a chuckle, but raised a smile anyway. She looked at Ethel, who was now smiling more broadly than ever, at her, before she asked Ethel, "Ethel. Dear Ethel. Would you like to see Mr. Daniels egg? Whilst we, Mr. Daniels and I, continue to discuss, what to you, is nothing more than a little local gossip. Which you're never to do. Gossip at all, that is!", said Alice.

This raised a large smile on Graeme's face. Ethel looked at Graeme's smiling face and then said, "Yes please, Mr. Daniels, I would like that very much indeed".

"I'll just get it for you then", continued Graeme, who looked inquiringly at Alice.

"If you would Mr. Daniels, and thank you very much on my daughter's behalf, once again", concluded Alice.

With that Graeme got up. Went to his shelvings, reached up, collected and brought the egg back to the table, handing it to Ethel, whilst he said, "Please be careful with it. It holds many memories for me, both of the past and present, and of my friends and colleagues, in or from, other towns and villages closeby".

"I will be", said Ethel, as she took the egg and began to examine it.

"The other thing is", said Alice, suddenly quite earnest as she replaced her cup into the saucer, "Is.....", she suddenly looked around the room, then out of the window, then leant forward and continued in a whisper, "They have special holidays or festivals. Sometimes yearly, or quarterly. One of them must be coming up or they've 'sight', in my opinion, and that's why they want you chased from this Heart's Hill, whatever is up there".

"Ooh", said Graeme, full of wonder. "I wonder why that might be. Not to you of course but to myself". He looked out.... out of his own window then, with a puzzled frown upon his face.

"So tell me", said Alice sharply. Suddenly sitting boldly upright in the chair, "What can you tell me of what I need to know? Of what goes on hereabouts? If I may make so bold a request?".

"Aye, you can now. You've a right too", said Graeme slowly and carefully, "You've given me food for thought and a lot more sense of some strange goings on, over the years, since my wife passed away to the other side".

"And what can you tell me?", prompted Alice, "Of the things I need to know. To help me to break this curfew of the Lord and Master, and to keep my child at school and out of the farmer's fields".

Ethel glanced up at this, as Alice leaned back into her chair and resumed drinking her tea. Ethel, herself, decided to do likewise, but found the tea unpleasant and unusual to her taste buds, thus resulting in her quickly placing the cup down and returning her attention, to the what she perceived as a magickal egg, full of patterns and mystery, of bright imagery and filled with a fondness of feeling which she felt internally, as she caressed the ornamental egg in both hands once more.

"Well now, I'll help you where I can, as I know you have to me, but I'll tell you no rumour or gossip, or things that maybe untrue, least I misguide you and do you a disservice", said Graeme.

"Agreed", said Alice, slightly annoyed inside.

"Well, let's see. The Lord, see? That be Lord Turner, but the Master be down at the farm", said Graeme.

Alice interupted, "Your meaning is still unclear".

Graeme paused at this. Took another sip of tea, then said, "Lord Turner owns most everything around here, see?".

"Yes", said Alice.

"He, as in Lord Turner, be the boss of most people, see?", continued Graeme.

"Why only most?", asked Alice, looking towards the window, but keeping one eye on Graeme.

"Well, Lord Turner owns the shops, they pay rent, see?". Alice nodded and Graeme continued, "He owns the mill and he pays the wages to the people that work there, who rent houses in his estate, or on his land, see?". Again Alice nodded.

"But farmer Guild runs the farm, pays his own wages, to his own workers, who normally live up on the Lord's land and pay rent to Lord Turner, see?", asked Graeme.

"I'm not sure I know your meaning", said Alice.

"Well, your master, if you work on the farm, is farmer Guild, but if you fall out of friends with Lord Turner, he may have you turfed out of your home, so only some people around here have a Lord and a Master, whilst most just have a Lord", explained Graeme.

"Aah", said Alice, now gazing fully out of the window, "Now I begin to understand".

She began to mall over this information, as Graeme continued, "The church and the police claim independence". Alice suddenly turned and stared Graeme in the eye, as he continued, "But it's the Hunter's Lodge were most local decisions get made".

Alice nodded at this, as Graeme continued, "May Day and New Year are celebrated at the village green. Farmer Guild occasionally attends, but the Lord's do not, but very little goes on in the area without the Lord or the Master, finding out, and there's devil's play afoot, when they both become involved", finished Graeme.

Alice finished her tea, thanked Graeme, whilst Ethel left her tea undrunk, but returned the egg with a courtesy. As they made to leave, Graeme commented, "It seems the weather has taken a turn for the worse".

Both Alice and Ethel looked at the sky, grey clouds could be seen moving towards them on the breeze they had felt before. Alice said, "I thank you for your hospitality and your help. I hope one day we meet again".

Graeme chuckled again, "Aye and I thank thee for your warnings, and I'll no hide from thee if you pass again", he said.

"Thank you and good-bye", said Alice, as she and Ethel set off from Graeme's home. They reached the road again and then Alice said to Ethel, "I think it may rain. I think it is best we go straight home. Maybe tomorrow we will go to the shop".

"Ok", said Ethel, and off they went, back from whence they came.

Chapter three

—•◦•—

BY THE TIME Alice and Ethel returned to their home, the sun had started to shine again. "I'll tell you what", said Alice to Ethel, "I'll make us a cup of tea and a sandwich each if you like?".

"Oh yes, oh yes, oh yes", said Ethel excitedly. "I'll go to my room to get re-dressed".

Alice painfully smiled, then looked at Ethel and said, "Yes, if you like. I'll call you down when it's ready, but please, take your time, I have a few things to sort out before I will be ready".

Ethel whooped with delight and ran up the stairs to her room, slamming the door behind her. Alice lit the stove, put the kettle on it, heaved a heavy sigh, then made towards the bread bin but changed her mind, and then sat gently upon one of the kitchen chairs, looked out the window and began to think.

'What can I do?', thought Alice, 'I'm new in the area and already, as I was in the last town I was in, forbidden by others to go out'. She felt a frown fall upon her. Lord Turner's words began to ring in her head, 'Control your child better', oh how could she do that? After all the trouble of yesterday, with Eric as well.

'Be a better wife! Oh Lord', she thought, 'It`s all this trouble with the move, and the upheaval on her child, Ethel'.

'Your child's future depends on your husband's performance at work', Ah! now that she understood, but how could she keep better control of Ethel, if, she, Alice, is not allowed out, or allowed into other's affairs?

As she mulled the problem over, the kettle began to boil. She made a pot of tea and two sandwiches, then called up the stairs to Ethel. Ethel came racing down the stairs.

Alice said, upon seeing the eagerness in Ethels eyes, "Calm down. I've made you a sandwich, and the tea has almost brewed. Please sit down, calm down, and then tell me what you learned today".

Ethel stopped in the doorway. Smiled, then walked all prim and proper to the kitchen table, where she sat herself down. Alice joined her at the table, and sat opposite to her, whilst taking a bite out of her sandwich.

Ethel took a small bite from her own sandwich, and started to chew slowly and speculatively gazed out of the window, for a few moments, whilst Alice poured out the tea, then said, "I learnt not to speak before a Lord, or else I will be punished", quite solemnly.

Alice half-choked on her sandwich momentarily, then raised her hand to cover her mouth, before half-smiling, and then she said, "Excuse me! My sandwich went down the wrong way".

"That's OK, no need to explain, I do it myself, once in a while", said Ethel more brightly, and then she, herself, tried to raise a smile.

Alice felt better at this, and said, "There's more. Something you've missed".

"What's that?", said Ethel, more brightly again, "Oh tell me! Oh tell me, what riddle is this?".

Alice smiled again. "You must speak when spoken too, and not before, when you are in the company of a Lord", she said.

"It's so not fair. I don't want to work on the farm", continued Ethel.

"Me neither, for you, but remember I got punished too", said Alice feeling mildly worse again.

"But what of Graeme, and his egg. What punishment did he get?", asked Ethel, annoyed now.

"None dear Ethel. None whatsoever. Only some friendly advice to take care", said Alice.

"Oh that's so unfair. Nobody even told me the rules", said Ethel.

"Oh but they did. I told you as we approached his cottage, to speak only when spoken too, or you would be packed off to the farm", scolded Alice, who then took another bite of her sandwich.

Ethel looked in conflict with herself for a few moments, then said, "Is one of those cups of tea for me?".

"Yes Ethel dear. You may take your pick. Whichever cup you choose, is the one which you shall drink , but, tell me, dear Ethel, why did you break your promise to me, and speak up, when not spoken too?", asked Alice, a little concernedly.

Ethel chose the cup closest to her right-hand side, and then said, "I'm confused now. You told me I should always ask when I am not sure of something".

"Yes, I know I did, but I asked you to promise me, for just a short while, not to speak unless spoken too. Why did you speak, dear Ethel, when not spoken too, and break your promise to me, the way you did, in front of the Lord?", asked Alice again.

Ethel gulped, took a sip of her tea, nibbled on her sandwich, and then gazed out of the window, whilst she tried to clear her mind.

"You do realise, do you not, that people who break promises are not well liked?", asked Alice, as she herself, began to sip her tea, feeling more in control of her own thoughts now.

Ethel turned from the window, looking older than her years, and then, accusingly said, "You said, 'Always', is all of the time. With no exception, or exceptions".

"Yes, that's correct. That's what I said, and that's what it is, but, and I truly mean this, a promise, is a promise, no matter what. You do have to understand that. It's the way of the world.

It's how we like it to be. It's the way it is. If you break your promises to me, irrespective of what I say, then I can, like your father now, that's true, no longer trust you.

"You tell me Ethel, if I can't trust you to keep a promise, what am I to do with you?", asked Alice

"I'll not work on the farm", said Ethel.

"Yes but, your father has disowned you. You cannot work at the mill, because you are an embarrassment. I cannot trust you to keep your word to me, no matter what I say, and all you can say is, 'I don't want to work on the farm'. Why is that? Why can't I trust you? And why won't you do as you are told?", asked Alice angrily.

Ethel thought for a moment, and then retorted, "And what does 'never', as in 'not at all', mean, if always means, only some of the time?".

Alice smiled and half-laughed. Took a bite out of her sandwich, and sat chewing slowly, looking out of the window, then up at the ceiling, and back and forth, until eventually, in a time that seemed an eternity to Ethel, she swallowed her food and then said, "It means the same as 'always', but in reverse".

"I made a mistake. I won't do it again, but you can still trust me. I'll say it again, but please don't send me to work on the farm. I don't want to spend my whole life working on the farm. Not even in the shop. Maybe I can work in the Post-Office, like Graeme, or in another shop, or even at Hunter's Lodge", said Ethel earnestly.

"Yes but I want you to be well-behaved. You are not well-behaved, for you broke your word, to me, and to no-one else, that I'm aware off", said Alice.

"Oh this is ridiculous", said Ethel angrily. She stood, as if to leave the room, but Alice interjected,

"Ethel, my Ethel. Tell me what you want? And I will get it for you, and I will end your curse....., and put a stop to this witchcraft, but you must trust me. There can be only one Ethel, and as my daughter, I will always do my best for you", said Alice. "Tell me, what do you want?".

"The egg", said Ethel. "I want Graeme's egg".

"Why dear Ethel? Why would you both want the egg?", asked Alice.

"I want.....", said Ethel slowly, then, "I want his home, and I want to live there, and I want him to do my work for me, because I do not want to work on the farm".

"Oh! My Ethel, can you explain, why the egg? Why does the egg hold such a fascination to you?", asked Alice.

"It's so pretty. I see so many patterns in it, and I forget the time while I gaze at it", said Ethel slowly.

"What is it's reverse Ethel? What if you have to live with Graeme? And have him physically look after you, what then?

"What if, dear Ethel, gets the egg, and you get the home and the body? Will you be able to cope? Will you be strong enough? Do you know what you want, enough to force through your will? Answer me, ye or nay, but never say you were not warned or told, that what you ask for, you will receive, and if you receive it, you may regret it, for all of your days", said Alice.

"I would like to live with Graeme. He seems ever so nice and friendly, but he did say, he wanted no interference in his life, or with whom he lived with", said Ethel.

"He meant physically dear, dear Ethel. I mean my Ethel. He never meant within the mind, or else he would have said so. That's the way it works. People say exactly what they mean, or they live with the consequences. Just as you two are now.

"Tell me you want this egg, or the reverse, and I can sort this out, and get you out of being in two minds. For you are my daughter, and unlike your father, I vowed before you were born, to do my best for you, in mind, or body, or in soul. You must believe me. It's totally true. A vow is like a promise, but promises can be broken, but a true vow, made from the heart of a womb, can never be broken, by folk such as me", said Alice.

Ethel went back to her sandwich. Taking nibble after nibble, chew after chew, interspersed with sips of tea. Occasionally looking out of the window, but mainly focusing her mind on her sandwich and tea. How had she come to this? Was interference only physical and not mental? And which one, her possessor or her, would win the body of an old man? Oh how neither of them wanted to work on the farm. It seems a dreadful place. She had crept down there the other day, to explore, past the, 'No trespassers', sign, whatever that meant, down to look at the animals, the fields and the workers, only to be left with a terrible feeling, but for life, her whole life, she was not sure she could agree to that, and her mother seemed, within her understanding, to be offering her a way out.

"Yes", said Ethel, "I agree. I either have his egg or his body".

"Bravo!", said Alice.

"Yes, yes, me too, me too, for I smell the blood of a feeble man", said Ethel, suddenly excited again.

"Agreed then", said Alice, who then pledged, "I will get that egg for you, no matter how long it takes me. No matter what I have to do to get it, and no matter whose affairs, except for the Lords and your father's, that I have to interfere with because, if a promise, is a promise, is a promise, more so than always or never, then a vow or an oath reigns to supreme, even to the law, in my opinion, just because you are my daughter of course", said Alice, feeling possessed, by the house again.

Chapter four

———◆•◆———

THE NEXT DAY, Ethel sat with Alice, drinking tea, after breakfast. Eric had already left for work. Ethel was brooding over where Heart's Hill was, and wondering if or when, she would be forced to work on the farm, when suddenly, Alice turned to her and said, "If it stays nice today, I will take you to see Mildred, and I can get my shopping from the local shop".

Ethel did not seem impressed. She looked blankly at Alice, but made no reply.

"I will introduce you to some local people, just as I promised", said Alice, trying to raise a smile and a happy tone.

Still no response from Ethel.

Alice tried again, "Look at me Ethel. You will have to speak to me eventually. You do know that. Even if your father will not tolerate you, and the local Lord thinks you are poorly behaved". She then softened her tone, as she noticed Ethel start to turn to look out of the window again. "I don't want to break my promise to you. You wouldn't like me to break my promise to you, would you?", she then suddenly asked.

Ethel turned back to look at Alice. "No", she said, "Not now I know I'm alone".

"Good", said Alice. "We might bring some goodies back with us", she continued, trying to raise Ethel's mood.

"Goodies!", said Ethel, suddenly looking excited, "What kind of goodies?".

Alice smiled at this. The panic was over. Ethel was speaking again.

"Oh tell me, oh tell me, oh tell me what goodies will we bring back?", asked Ethel excitedly.

Alice laughed, "Oh Ethel, you're so funny at times", she said quite callously.

"Oh tell me, oh tell me, will we have any eggs? Oh any eggs at all, even ones which aren't gold?", asked Ethel.

Alice was alarmed at this. "Now calm down a minute, please, explain to me what you mean, if I may make so bold to ask?", she said.

Ethel smiled, then said, "But I am to tell no-one, what I saw or heard yesterday. Even you must understand I cannot explain what I mean".

Ethel waited for a reply. Alice gazed out of the window, what had she said yesterday that had drawn such a response. "Can you explain, just a little bit more?", asked Alice.

Ethel gulped. "Maybe an extra cup of tea will help. It does with me", said Alice.

Alice smiled, topped up both their cups with more tea, and then said, "You can tell me, for I was there, but not Graeme, for that's not fair. After all, you can only trust me now, but you are never to speak of it, unless I ask, and we are alone, in our house, drinking tea, with all the doors and windows shut, but not locked. Then, and only then, can you speak, and no matter what else, I will keep you…".

Just then, there was a knock at the door. Alice's smile froze on her face for an instant. The knock came again. Ethel looked towards the front door.

Alice said quickly, "Hush child, don't make a sound. Don't make a move. They will go in a minute or two".

"Yoo-hoo", came a call, "Please answer the door. It's only me, Mildred. I just decided to call".

"Hush", said Alice urgently to Ethel, who had started twitching in her seat.

"I know you're in there. It's only me. Mildred from the mill. I've brought you some bread. Moira from down the road said that she's not seen you go out", came the callers call again.

"Oh wake up Ethel. Don't be scared, but tired. Try not to cry and speak only when spoken too", said Alice, quietly but urgently. Ethel rubbed her eyes, "What's going on?", she asked, as she stretched her arms upward.

"There's someone at the door", said Alice, as another knock came, "Be quiet, whilst I get it".

"Ok", said Ethel.

"Coming", called out Alice, as she rose from her kitchen seat, to answer the door.

She opened the front door, only to be confronted by an iratated Mildred. "Hello Mildred. Can I help you?", asked Alice calmly.

"Oh! I'm terribly sorry to intrude, but I've brought some bread around for you, from Eric", said Mildred, with a big smile.

"Oh thank you", said Alice. "Here, let me take it from you. I'm terribly busy at the moment".

"Yes, I know, or I presume so, because I've been at the door for quite a while, but Eric has asked me to check in on Ethel, on his behalf", said Mildred.

"Ethel?", said Alice alarmedly, "Whatever for?".

"Lord Turner called in at the mill. He called Eric to his office, apparently he asked if he had, well….. I'm not sure how to say this, but, been a little rude, or too harsh on Ethel, only yesterday, whilst he was about his business in the area", said Mildred.

"Oh my goodness! Whatever gave him that idea?", asked Alice sternly.

"Well, that's why he spoke to Eric, but Eric knew nothing about it", said Mildred.

"Oh my", said Alice, "I truly am very busy today though".

"Oh dear, of course it's none of my affair what goes on in your home, or the affairs between you and your husband, or daughter.....", said Mildred.

"Oh please", said Alice quickly, looking up and down the road. "You'd better step into the hallway".

As Alice backed away the door and Mildred made to step in, Mildred continued, "But it's Lord Turner, you see? He may have to leave town for a day or two, and he doesn't want it praying on his mind, so he's asked Eric for a report, but Eric's ever so busy, what with the continuing emergency at the mill, so he's asked for my opinion on the matter, so he can tell Lord Turner, exactly what he knows about it".

"Well I don't know if I like the idea of that", said Alice with a gulp.

"Well, either Lord Turner will turn up himself, and it will get Eric into trouble at the mill, or Eric will have to borrow a horse and cart, and race over to here, and back, and you wouldn't like that now, would you?", asked Mildred.

"You'd better speak to her then. I've no wish to hold my day up, awaiting for his Lordship or for Eric, to be withdrawn from his duties, for the sake of a quick word or two", said Alice.

"Just a few questions for Ethel any possible explanation, if one is due. Of that you can be sure", said Mildred.

"This way", said Alice, then gently calling into the kitchen, "Ethel, there is someone here to see you. Make yourself....".

Mildred interupted there, "That won't be necessary. I'll take it from here, least it cause more confusion than is necessary, thus taking up more of your time".

Alice looked glum, but led Mildred into the kitchen, regardless.

"Would you like me to take your bread for you?", asked Alice.

"Thank you", said Mildred, passing the bread to Alice, then she said to Ethel, "Hello Ethel".

Ethel stared blankly at Mildred. Alice said, "I'll make a pot of tea, if you like?", to Mildred.

"Yes, thank you dear", said Mildred to Alice. Ethel smiled at this. Encouraged, Mildred said, "My name is Mildred. I work at the mill, with your father, Eric".

Ethel continued to stare at Mildred, whilst Alice set about heating up some water.

"Do you mind if I sit beside you for a while?", asked Mildred to Ethel. Ethel shook her head in the negative. "I am speaking to you. You do know that, don't you?", asked Mildred.

This time Ethel nodded affirmatively, so Mildred sat beside her.

"You can speak to me, because I am speaking to you. You do know that, don't you?", continued Mildred. Ethel once again nodded her agreement. "Ok", said Mildred, "Then I should tell you, most folk expect you to speak to them, when you are spoken to", she continued.

Alice dropped a cup, which made a cluttering sound, but failed to smash. "Oops! Silly me," said Alice.

"Oh that's Ok", said Mildred soothingly. "It's your cup, and at least it's not broken". Alice smiled wryly and then bent down to retrieve the cup.

"Some folk, especially the Lord you spoke with the other day", continued Mildred to Ethel, "Will even punish you, if you do not speak to them, when spoken to", she concluded, with her own wry smile to Ethel.

Ethel smiled back this time, to Mildred, but still remained quiet. "I", said Mildred quite authoritively, "Would like you, for one, to speak to me, whenever I speak to you. Do you understand?", asked Mildred.

Ethel nodded at this.

"Your father, for another, would like you to speak back to him, when he speaks to you, as well. Do you understand?", asked Mildred again. Once again, Ethel nodded.

Then Mildred continued, more sternly now, "But Lord Turner, from the other day, who you met briefly, demands that you speak, not only to him and to me, but to your father as well, whenever we speak to you, even if it is only to say, 'I don't know', or, 'I can't rightly say'. Am I making myself clear to you Ethel?", asked Mildred, but still Ethel just stared at her and said nothing.

Alice interposed, gently at first, "You'd better do as they say, Ethel. They really will have you working on the farm, if you don't do as they say".

Ethel looked confused at this. Mildred shot a glance at Alice, who looked out of the window, almost instantly, and then turned back to the stove.

This caused Mildred to glower mildly, at Alice's back, before she turned back to Ethel and said, "Lord Turner said you would only work on the farm, if you started to learn about witchcraft".

"But.....", said Ethel, quickly, almost urgently, before lapsing into a tight-lipped silence, again.

"But what Ethel? Can you tell me? Please, what the matter is?" asked Mildred. Ethel went to gazing out of the window. Alice slammed the kettle down, and once again said,

"Oops!".

"Can you shed any light upon this matter, Alice?", asked Mildred unexpectedly.

Alice turned from the stove quickly. She glowered at Mildred openly. Then she said, "I, like my daughter Ethel, here, are both forbidden from speaking about this matter, at his Lordship's insistence, request and demand, even though it appears to be the talk of the village and the mill, not only to my eyes, but probably to yours and everybody elses, as well".

Mildred sat in shock. Not only at Alice's vehemence, but also at what seemed, a more tricky task to her, than she first thought.

At that, the water boiled. Alice made a fresh pot of tea, and brought clean cups and saucers to the table, from where she removed both Ethel's and her own, previous cups, before seating herself down, facing Mildred this time.

Mildred, calmly turned to Ethel once more, and said gently, "I'll ask you again Ethel, do you understand that you are not to work on the farm, unless you learn about witchcraft and curses, as the Lord said?", asked Mildred.

They sat in silence for a while. Ethel gazed out of the window. Alice eventually poured out three cups of tea. Mildred and Alice occasionally glanced at each other, before Ethel eventually said, "But my mother wants to take me around the village".

"What`s wrong with that Ethel?", asked Mildred, mildly perturbed. Ethel stayed looking out of the window. Eventually Mildred, after sipping some tea, asked Alice, "Can you shed any light on this for me yet? You don't want a fuss over all of this, do you? Not so soon after arriving here, from whence you came. You are still quite new to most people's, hereabouts".

Alice slowly looked towards Mildred. "I can't say, what I don't know", she said.

"Are you scaring this child? If I've a mind to ask. So as I know if I'm wasting my time here or not, when, similar to yourself, so you say, I or we, both have better things to do?", said Mildred, mildly stern.

Alice spoke defensively, "I've no idea what's wrong with taking Ethel around the village, to meet people. That's all I said".

Mildred turned to Ethel, "What's wrong with going out around the village Ethel? Can you tell me that? For arguements sake or debate, just so I can understand, a little?".

Ethel gulped. Alice took a long sip of tea, and Ethel reached out for her own cup, and took a long sip as well, before placing the cup back down, and saying, "I'm not sure".

"Please, sit and think for a while. Drink some tea if you choose, but please try to explain yourself a little bit more", said Mildred.

Alice made to speak, but Mildred interjected quickly, "Hush. Let Ethel. Try not to get mixed up in this affair", then turned and smiled at Ethel, who, in return, kept silent but smiled back, in return.

Eventually Ethel said, "I don't know the names of the local places, and where not to go".

Mildred puzzled over this, then asked Alice, "Is there any reason, that either comes to mind or that you can speak of, as to why this may be relevant to Ethel? That you can speak of? If I may ask for your input on this matter?".

"None that I know off", remarked Alice.

"Well Ethel", said Mildred, pointedly to Ethel, "If you are asked, as you will be I'm sure, if you have any questions, that you start to ask the names of things or places, instead of asking for rhymes all the time".

Ethel smiled at this and looked at Alice, who returned the smile. Alice made to speak, but Mildred quickly interjected, "Ah now! Alice, I hope you will stay out of this affair".

Alice frowned and lowered her head. All three of them took a drink from their cups and then replaced their cups.

Mildred gulped, and then asked, "Did Lord Turner upset you yesterday, Ethel?".

"A little", confessed Ethel.

"He sends his apologies for speaking so abruptly to you. He had, in his opinion, very important business to attend too. He has told your father, he does not expect you to work on the farm, as long as you steer clear of witchcraft and cursing people", explained Mildred slowly, and then she asked, "Do you understand that?".

"Yes", said Ethel with a gulp.

"Can you accept the apology of Lord Turner, for the abrupt way he spoke to you?", asked Mildred.

"Yes", said Ethel.

"No hard feelings between you and Lord Turner then, is there?", asked Mildred

"No", responded Ethel glumly.

"Maybe one day your father will take you around the village and tell you the names of everywhere", said Mildred, with a sweet smile for Ethel, who shot a look at Alice, who was sat upright in her chair, eyes wide open, but her lips were firmly closed.

"Maybe he will, one day", admitted Ethel, more glumly than before.

"That's the spirit dear, I know your father's very busy nowadays, but he does think very highly of you at the moment, and he does always have time to chat to you, so he tells me", said Mildred, smiling broadly.

They sat in silence for a while. Finished their tea, and then Mildred said, "Ethel dear, do you have any questions about what I said?".

Alice motioned toward the stove, but Mildred motioned for her to stop.

"No", said Ethel firmly.

"I'm pleased about that", said Mildred and then she added, "Is there any message I can pass on to your father for you, about the matter?".

Ethel looked at Alice, who once again looked tight-lipped, returned her gaze to Mildred and replied, "No, but please thank him for his concern on the matter".

"I will do. Thank you for your time Ethel", Ethel nodded at this, as Mildred rose from the table and then spoke to them both, "I must be leaving, for the day is young, and I have much to do".

"Thank you Mildred", said Alice. "For clearing up the matter, on my daughter's behalf".

"My pleasure", responded Mildred, "And I thank thee for the tea and the hospitality".

As they reached the door, Alice concluded, "My pleasure. Please always feel welcome to call again, even if it is only for a chat or some tea. I get so little company, what with the cottage being isolated, but next to the farm".

"I shall do", waved Mildred, as she walked down the path.

Alice returned to the kitchen, with a light gait. "Shall we go out then? This afternoon? We can talk on the way to the shop, but you must be careful what you say, when and if, we meet anybody on the way", she asked Ethel.

"Yes", said Ethel. "But only to where we have been before".

"Why's that then Ethel?", chided Alice, "Why suddenly so scared?".

"I want to avoid places of witchcraft and curses, that's all", said Ethel, trying to sound stern.

"Oh, really?", replied Alice. "I hadn't thought of that before".

Ethel looked glum. Alice chuckled inwardly. "Ok", she said, "I'll make you a promise, Ethel, if you'd like me too?".

"What would the promise be, before I agree?", asked Ethel, quite interested suddenly.

"I would make you the promise that I would not or will not, today at least, take you to any place of witchcraft or curses, but only to the shop at the mill. Past the knight's cottage and Graeme's too", said Alice beguilingly, "But only if you agree to walk with me, and speak freely as we walk together down the road, when that is, we two are alone with no-one else in view".

Ethel smiled and said, "Yes, I would like that".

"Then it's agreed", said Alice, "I'll do some housework, the dishes too, and change my clothes, and then we can go for our walk", she finished.

"Ok", said Ethel briskly, "I will go to my room and prepare myself".

With this, she jumped up and trotted out of the kitchen and up the stairs.

Alice heard Ethel's bedroom door close, and then she set about clearing the kitchen table.

Chapter five

A SHORT WHILE later, they set out for their walk. The sun was still shining, as it was the day before. The world looked bright to Ethel. Small white fluffy clouds, moved lazily across the sky.

As they walked alongside farmer Guild's field, Ethel asked, "Will Graeme give me the egg today?", of Alice.

Alice's head fell backwards, as she laughed out loud. Then she said, "Oh Ethel dear, it doesn't work like that".

Ethel frowned, and then replied, "I'm not dear Ethel. I'm your Ethel. Your baby Ethel. Please get her out of my mind".

Alice stopped laughing, and said, "I'm sorry Ethel. I didn't realise you knew, but, I'll tell you what, I ask him if he'll gift it to you".

Ethel became excited. "Oh yes! Oh yes! Oh yes! It's a gift. Oh please ask him to sell it, to me as a gift", she rhymed.

Alice frowned, then said, "Umm, I did say it was your game, didn't I?".

"Oh yes, oh yes, it's a wonderful game. Oh please let him name his own price for his home", said Ethel.

Alice said, "I'm not sure I understand you now, but I'll do as you ask, but try not to speak, unless you are spoken to, and then only to answer the question you're asked".

"How hard should I try? Should I truly not pry? Oh why? Oh why? Do I sing when I cry?", said Ethel.

"I'd like you to know", said Alice, "I'm not allowed to intrude. For my beliefs are not Lord Turner's, but I made you a promise and I will keep my word, but you'll have to advise me how to play the game of a devil", finished Alice.

Ethel laughed. "I like it when you rhyme. For I know it's not a crime, but a devil I'll not be, for you called me a ghost or a spirit", said Ethel with a smile and a glance.

Alice smiled, looked back at Ethel, gulped and then said, "Try as hard as you like. For it does no harm, but if Lord Turner turns up, you may be in trouble. Hush now. We are approaching the knight's cottage. Try to be polite, if they are about".

They continued to walk along the road. They could both see Moira and Philip in the garden. They looked at each other and smiled, before they reached them.

"Good morning to you both", called out Alice, to the knight's.

Philip looked up first, from his task of weeding, and then Moira turned from her pruning, as well. "Good morning to both of you again", said Philip.

"Oh don't mind Philip, though it may be true what he says", said Moira, who then asked, "And what can we do for you?".

"Maybe true?", questioned Philip, turning to face Moira. "But even you agreed earlier, it was a good morning, if I'm not mistaken".

"Oh Philip, you can never prove that", said Moira, "But it's a good job we're married and I can't contest what you say, in court, if I've a mind".

Philip laughed at this. Shook his head from side to side, and then said, "And that's why I love you my dear, because we're together, for better or for worse".

"I'm just passing through. I thought I'd trouble you, just so you know that I passed through", said Alice with a smile.

"Has your child found a job yet?", asked Philip, in surprise.

"Not yet", said Alice.

"It's nice for us to live this side of the river", said Moira.

"Aye", agreed Philip. "Some folks around here, thinks we're the toll-gate, similar to that, t'other side of Heart's Hill", he said with a wry smile.

Ethel froze!

"Not that we get paid or ought though", continued Moira, "If you take my meaning?".

"Aye", said Alice. "I think I do now, but what of you Moira? Does your husband speak true? Is it a good morning to you?", asked Alice.

"It was when I said, of that I'll admit, but I get asked too many questions to admit anything else", said Moira.

Alice fell silent at this.

"Where's Heart's hill?", interjected Ethel, into the new silence.

All three turned to stare at her. Eventually, Philip said, "Why? It's over yonder", pointing to a range of hills, in a south-westerly direction, then he added, "But you can't see it from here, see?".

"Thank you", said Ethel.

"How about you dear?", asked Moira to Ethel, "What would you like to do?".

"Oh aye! Are you working at the farm yet?", asked Graeme to Ethel.

"No I'm not", said Ethel resolutely. "And I hope one day to work at the mill, like my father does".

"Oh, hush child", said Alice.

"Oh he does, does he?", said Philip.

"Oh Philip, don't push the child. She may say something she'll regret", said Moira, then she continued, "But what would you like today, then?", to Ethel.

"I'd like an egg", said Ethel.

"Really?", said Philip, very confused.

"She means an egg of Graeme's", said Alice.

47

"Oh dear", said Moira to Alice, "You really shouldn't get involved".

Alice looked from Philip to Moira, but remained silent again.

Philip heaved a deep breath, and said, "Oh Graeme, there's not much I can say about Graeme".

"We've not seen him today, dear, if that's what you mean?", said Moira.

Ethel shook her head from side to side.

"He goes to the lodge, see? Not like me. I know my place, see? I goes to the inn, don't I dear?", said Philip.

"Oh yes, it's true", said Moira. "Philip always goes the inn, and I go to the church occasionally, but Graeme goes to the lodge", finished Moira dramatically.

"Aye!", said Philip. "Hunter's lodge, over yonder", he turned and pointed north-westerly, and concluded, "Behind Turner's mansion, practically, from here".

"Hunter's Lodge?", queried Alice, "What is this place?".

"Ah, well, I've never been there, see? Maybe Moira can explain", said Philip.

"Well ….. It's close to church …… but …. ?", said Moira.

"But what?", said Alice, intrigued.

Silence!

"Is it cursed?", asked Ethel, suddenly, unexpectedly.

"Oh good grief", said Moira.

"Oh Lord, no!", exclaimed Philip, "Lord Turner goes there occasionally, but not very often".

"He, his Lordship, steers clear of cursed places", said Moira.

"Really?", said Alice.

"Aye, but…..", said Philip.

"Yes, really", interjected Moira, "He is a very respectable man. He has no time or money for witches or curses".

"But what, Philip?", asked Alice.

All three turned to look at Philip.

Philip stood up from his position, "Aye, well, if I say ought more, I may be doing a disservice, not to Lord Turner, but to some of the places he goes, whether he knows or not. For some people, so they tell me in the inn, say that Turner's mill is cursed, as are all the people who work there", said Philip.

"Oh, goodness gracious!", exclaimed Alice.

"I'm not going there. Never! Do you hear me?", ranted Ethel to Alice.

"Oh please calm down. Everybody calm down", called Moira.

All three chorused, "But!".

Almost all together, but Moira continued, speaking over them all, "The local Priest has assured us all the curse has been lifted, for those that go to church occasionally. Though probably not for the fools who go and spend their money in the inn, just so the owner can spend the proceeds in the Lodge".

"Aye, well, it's better than spending it in the church, dear", said Philip.

"Oh please Philip", interjected Alice. "Not in front of Ethel. Please save your discussion on this matter for another time".

"But what of the curse?", asked Ethel.

"Aye, well ……", said Philip.

"Oh hush Philip. Please don't speak of curses to Ethel. Neither of these two go to the church and neither go to the inn", said Moira.

"We'll stay out of the mill Ethel dear. There is no need for us to go there today", said Alice.

"I will not work on the farm", said Ethel, sternly now.

"What about the mill?", asked Moira, "Would you like to work at the mill or the inn?".

Ethel thought for a moment or two. Alice looked about to speak, but then went tight-lipped.

"Aye", said Philip, "We'll let you think on that one for a while, though I'm surprised you don't want to work on the farm".

Ethel remained silent.

"Well, we'll be on our way today. Thank you both for your advice and your time of day", said Alice.

"Goodday to you both", said Moira.

"Aye, have a pleasant day", said Philip.

They waved each other off. As Alice and Ethel walked down the road, crossed the bridge, and drew level with Craggy Tor. Then Alice said, "Maybe I would rethink what job I would like to do, if I were you, but the choice is entirely up to you".

Ethel smiled, almost painfully, "Yes, I need to learn more, before I make a decision. Maybe Graeme knows more about the Lodge, than Philip and Moira".

"Umm", said Alice. "I hadn't thought of that".

They continued down the road. Turned into the road, leading to the mill, in silence now, and saw Graeme's cottage up on the left-hand side of the road.

As they approached, they saw Graeme was speaking to someone, over his garden wall. They stopped talking as they spotted Alice and Ethel, turned, and waved. Both Alice and Ethel, waved back in return.

"Be good Ethel, remember it's Graeme", said Alice, quietly.

They soon recognised Mildred. As they came within earshot, Alice greeted them, "Good morning to you Graeme, and to you again Mildred".

"Good morning Alice, and to you, too, Ethel", said Graeme.

"Good morning to the two of you again", said Mildred, "I see that you are taking a walk today".

"Oh yes! Tis a beautiful day. I thought we would go to the shop, by the mill", said Alice.

"Oh you should have said. I could have picked up and delivered to you, whatever goods you wanted", said Mildred, with a wry smile.

"Where's the shop?", asked Ethel.

Graeme chuckled, Mildred threw him a frown, then she smiled again, and said, "You just have to follow this road around

Craggy Tor, and you will arrive at it. It's just before you arrive at Turner's mill".

"Oh thank you", said Ethel, looking relieved.

Alice half-smiled at this, and then said, "I promised Ethel I'd take her to see some of the village, and I thought I'd get my shopping anyway, whilst we were out for the day, but thank you for the thought, and the offer of help".

"It's my pleasure to be of help to you and your family", responded Mildred, "But please, never be frightened of asking for my help".

"How are you today, Graeme?", asked Alice to Graeme.

"I'm very well thank you, and pleased to be in the sunshine, if you don't mind me saying so", replied Graeme.

"Oh, that's nice", said Alice.

"Ethel tells me you have a wonderous egg, Graeme", said Mildred. "Maybe I could see it as well?".

"Oh did she now?", asked Graeme, "And what else did she say? If I may be so bold as to ask?".

Mildred laughed and Alice lowered her head to look at the ground. Graeme looked squarely at Ethel, who then admitted, "That's all I said. Honestly! Not an extra word than that".

"Oh, is that right?", asked Graeme of Alice, who looked up and said,

"Yes. That's correct Graeme. Maybe you would like to sell the egg to me, so I can give it to Ethel?".

Graeme smiled sadly, "I would not like to sell my memories", he said

"Then maybe as a gift. Maybe you could gift it to Ethel?", asked Alice.

"I'll no be gifting my memories away", said Graeme.

"Oh please, have a heart Graeme. Where's your charity and good will?", said Mildred, challengingly.

"This is nought to do with you, Mildred. Mind your own business. This is not church business", said Graeme.

"Oh please, oh please, oh please Graeme. Leave your memories with me. I'll come and live with you, in your old age. Take care of you and keep you company", said Ethel, excitedly.

"Eh?", asked Graeme, but before he could continue, Alice said,

"Oh Graeme, she's too young to understand. Please forgive my daughter's impetuousness", said Alice.

Mildred quickly interjected, "Oh an engagement present. You could have a new wife when she comes of age. Oh wouldn't that be exciting news to spread on your round".

"Now don't be bringing my job into this Mildred", said Graeme sharply.

"Oh yes, oh yes, oh yes", said Ethel, "All for the love of a golden egg", excitedly.

"Have you put her up to this?", asked Graeme, sharply of Alice.

"I've not mentioned it, have I dear Ethel?", asked Alice.

"Oh no, oh no, not to me. He-he!", said Ethel.

"Then I will accept your child's apology, on your behalf", said Graeme to Alice.

"But Graeme, she's not allowed to interfere", said Mildred.

"What?", said Graeme sharply, to Mildred.

"Then it's agreed!", stated Ethel, jumping up and down.

"Well it's difficult to explain", said Mildred.

"No its not", said Graeme irately, and then resolutely added, "I'll not gift thee my egg. Not my wife's memories".

"We'll see about that Graeme", said Mildred. "Charity starts at home. It's time you remembered people have to move on. Your wife's memories as well".

"You…..? You put her up to this?", asked Graeme of Mildred.

"I'll not admit to what I know nought about", said Mildred with a smile.

"Then it's agreed", stated Ethel more sternly.

"I'll no gift away my egg, and my home, for someone more than half my age, by the time I come to marry them, and....", said Graeme, before being interupted by Mildred,

"Oh Graeme, she's not said she'll marry you. Only that she might become your maid", said Mildred sternly.

"Aye, that's true", said Graeme.

Before he could continue, Ethel said, "Then it's true, that you need someone to look after you, in your old age?".

Graeme gulped and said, "I can look after myself. Not only now, but in the future. I can choose my own help, if I need any, but if the young lady wants to be a maid, then she can apply at the mansion of Lord Turner when she's of age. Maybe he will employ her, and for a wage. Not an egg, if you take my drift?".

Mildred said, "But Graeme, you're nearing retirement age. You need to plan ahead. Just like on your round".

Graeme sighed. "I'll not be forced into discussing my retirement plans. I have told you this before Mildred", said Graeme.

"Oh Graeme, I have to agree, but maybe you can tell Ethel about the Lodge, if you would be so kind", requested Alice.

"And why would I be so kind as to do that then?", asked Graeme.

All three turned to face Alice.

Alice said, quite bemusedly, "Oh I'm sure Ethel will agree. Philip knight, the husband of Moira, from down by the bridge, has asked Ethel if she has found a job yet, and he did say, and Moira agreed, that you may be able to tell Ethel about the Lodge, that's the only reason I ask. Honestly".

"Oh, that be Hunter's Lodge then. Aye, it's a friendly enough place. Built for the gentry originally, but used as a place for meetings and refreshments, for local shopowners, landowners and government workers like myself. Sometimes and on occasion, Master Guild and Lord Turner attend the Lodge, for meetings and discussions. If there are any jobs over there, you had best attend a seminar, and ask what you can do", said Graeme proudly.

"Oh it's a devil of a place", said Mildred, but then on seeing Ethel's response said, "But not cursed of course. All the decent folks around here go to the church, or the inn. That's the way of things around here, but a job is a job, of course".

Ethel smiled at this.

"Thank you on my daughter's behalf, once again Graeme", stated Alice.

"Then it's agreed?", asked Ethel, looking at all three of them in turn.

"Is what agreed?", asked Graeme, somewhat reluctantly.

"Yes dear Ethel. It's a possibility you can attend a seminar, at the Lodge one day. I'm sure Graeme may vouch for your enthusiasm, if nothing else", said Alice.

"Aye! That I might, as well", said Graeme, almost flippantly.

"Well, we must be on our way to the shop. I'll bid thee both a goodday", said Alice.

"I'll accompany you, if you like? If Ethel doesn't object", said Mildred.

"I don't object", said Ethel.

"Goodday to you all then", said Graeme, as he returned to his gardening chores.

With that, Mildred, Alice and Ethel, all set off to the shop.

Chapter six

As THEY WALKED down the road, they passed another cottage.

"Who lives there?", inquired Alice of Mildred.

"That's the home of the Welsh family. They work at the mansion. We local people seldom see them", said Mildred, "I'm not sure though, if they speak to Graeme or not. Apparantly they say he talks to plants, in his garden".

"Really?", said Alice, quite surprised.

"Yes, really! You should ask them, but probably Susan really, she said she caught him speaking to them one day. He was very embarrassed, denied it of course, very politely, but couldn't say who he was speaking to, apparently", said Mildred with a smile.

"Oh the poor man. He must be ever so lonely", said Alice.

"Yes, he's never been too popular, but less so since his wife passed away", said Mildred.

"Why so?", asked Alice.

"The two of them never mixed with anyone locally", replied Mildred.

"What's that over there?", asked Ethel suddenly.

Before them, the road swung to the right, but beyond that, at the base of two hills, sat a large pond or a small lake. As they neared, the murky waters waters appeared brown, riddled with bushes and trees all around. A few ducks floated on the pond, as they sat in the shade of the hills from the late morning sun.

"That", said Mildred, "Is Turner's pond". She didn't look impressed with the pond. Ethel, expected more information on the pond, but found none was forthcoming.

Alice spoke into the silence, "Has it been there long?".

"As long as I remember", said Mildred, gloomily.

They reached the turn of the road, a small footpath led down to the pond from the edge of the road. Alice looked towards Ethel and said, "Maybe one day, if you like, we can bring some food for the ducks, if you've a mind to feed them".

Ethel smiled, "Yes, that might be nice", then glowered suddenly and said, "But I'm not too sure I'd like that now".

"It is farm work", agreed Mildred, "Feeding the animals".

Alice looked dumb-founded, as they passed by Turner's pond, and saw in front of them a row of houses on the right-hand side of the road, with the shop on the other-side. The mill was just in sight, at the far end of the stretch of the road, before it veered to the left, and up Isop mountain.

"That's the mill up ahead", said Mildred, "With the high wall surround".

"Yes I know", said Alice. "I have been there, when we came to the area".

"What's it's curse?", asked Ethel quickly.

This drew both Alice and Mildred's attention. They shot a look at Ethel, who looked straight ahead at the mill, then at each other.

Alice shrugged.

Mildred heaved a sigh. She looked at the mill, looked back, and found both Ethel and Alice staring at her, as if waiting for a reply. "I don't know of any curse at the mill", she admitted, reluctantly at first, and then felt more resolve fill her, "But irrespective of that, I live over here, on the right. The second cottage along. We've been here quite a while".

There was a row of four cottages. White fronts, slate roofs, with two chimney stacks, and brown wooden doors and windows.

"They look very pretty", remarked Alice.

They passed the cottages and entered the shop. A little bell rang as the door opened. Ethel smiled at this. There was an assortment of breads, pastry's, grain, eggs and cereal in the shop. Ethel was quite impressed.

"Mrs. Baker, are you there? It's Mildred. I've got Eric's wife and daughter with me", called out Mildred, into the empty shop.

"I'll be out in a minute or so. Please look around", called back Mrs. Baker.

Alice got out her shopping list and began to look around. Suddenly the door opened to a new tinkling of the bell, and in marched a man, covered in flour, from head to foot. White flour!

"Hello Sam", said Mildred.

"Oh, goodday to you Mildred. I've been sent to the shop to see if Mrs. Baker has all her requirements for tonight's baking", said Sam.

Mildred turned to Alice, "And this is Alice, Eric's wife".

"Goodday to you Alice", responded Sam.

"And this is their daughter Ethel", continued Mildred.

"Goodday to you Miss", responded Sam.

"And a goodday to you all. I'm Mrs. Baker, for those of you new to my shop, and do not already know me", said Mrs. Baker, who had appeared at the counter at the back of the shop.

"Goodday to you Mrs. Baker, and to you as well Sam", said Alice, as she continued to look around.

"What know you of a curse on the mill Sam? For the little one here", asked Mildred.

"Me?", questioned Sam, slightly surprised, "I know nothing. Nothing at all in fact, to be totally frank and honest about it".

"I was speaking to Graeme earlier", continued Mildred, "What do you know of him? As he may need a maid in his old age, apparently".

"What?", answered Sam, "That old kook. I'll know he'll retire soon, but he holds his wife's memories in some kind of egg, so I hear".

Alice shot a glance at Ethel. Ethel stood staring at Sam. Mildred glanced around the room, only to see Mrs. Baker nodding, watching them all, with a stern expression on her face. Mildred continued, "What else? For arguements sake".

"Umm", said Sam, thinking hard, then added, "Whilst I think he is OK, some folks were unhappy, so I hear, that he sent his wife's body back to Thorberry, to be buried. Kind of makes them think unkindly of him, in my opinion".

"I don't know what's wrong with the women around here", said Mrs. Baker suddenly, "Him going all the way to Thorberry for a wife, while there's good honest women around here, still waiting to be married. Honesty! I truly don't".

"Is he truly a widower then?", asked Alice.

"Oh aye! You can be sure of that. We had all sorts of folk from Thorberry coming here, when she died. Asking all sorts of queer questions. Some trouble so I heard, but none that I can speak off", said Sam.

"He speaks to his plants, so I've been told", stated Mrs. Baker, "Honest to goodness! I've no idea why he would want to do that", she said, shaking her head in dismay.

Egged on by this, Sam said, "Aye! Well, some folks say his wife's soul lives on in his egg". Ethel jumped at this, but Sam continued, "And he talks to that as well, and that's why he had her buried in Thorberry, but, that's only hearsay of course", he said heatedly.

"Now calm down Sam. We don't want a fight about it, or any more folks from Thorberry coming over here, trying to find out what's going on", said Mildred.

"But they already are", said Sam, "In my opinion. People have been spotted, far end of Isop hill and Heart's Hill".

At this, Alice dropped a bag of flour that she was holding and spun around quickly, then said, "Ooh! I'm terribly sorry Mrs. Baker. I think the bag has split open".

"Oh, don't worry about that Alice. You pick another and I'll put it on your husband's slate", said Mrs. Baker.

Alice stared for a moment, then said, "Oh! Thank you Mrs. Baker".

"Tell me about these folk Sam", said Mrs. Baker. "Who's been seeing them?".

"Oh, I'm not sure now. I think Lord Turner is looking into it. Nought to do with us, or the police. They ain't done nothing wrong, up to now, but it's still Lord Turner's Land".

"Thank you Sam. I have all I need for tonight's baking", said Mrs. Baker.

"Aye, well, I'll bid thee all a goodday then, and I'll be off, back to the mill", said Sam, who then tilted his cap and left the shop, to the tinkling of the bell on the door.

"Nice man Sam. Lives two doors down from me, with his mother and father still. Get's a little bit excited at news of strangers though", said Mildred, with a small shake of her head.

"Can I take these please? Mrs. Baker?", asked Alice. Producing a pile of goods on the counter, behind which was an open doorway into the living quarters.

"I'll just make a note of them first", said Mrs. Baker, producing a large ledger from under the counter, and turning the pages slowly. Then she said, slowly, "It's the Dale Ghoul in my opinion".

"What is? Mrs. Baker, what is the Dale Ghoul?", asked Mildred, puzzledly.

"Graeme!", Mrs. Baker continued. "If he talks to ought that's not there, it'll be the Dale Ghoul".

"Who's the Dale Ghoul?", asked Ethel, feeling confused.

Mildred and Alice chuckled. "Ooh!", said Mrs. Baker, "The Dale Ghoul is one of those ancient Gods of the forest and trees, so I've been told".

"It's a little bit more than that Mrs. Baker, as well you know", said Mildred.

"Well, whether it's a devil or a spirit", continued Mrs. Baker, only to be interupted by Ethel, who shrieked,

"Aaaargh!", and then clasped her hands over both of her ears.

"Oh please Mrs. Baker stop. You'll be giving Ethel nightmares", said Alice suddenly.

"Oh very well, but she shouldn't ask such questions, if she doesn't want to hear the answers, in my opinion", said Mrs. Baker.

Alice went to soothe Ethel, who was beginning to look alarmed, "Calm down Ethel", said Alice, "We'll be leaving in a minute or two, all being well".

Mildred and Mrs. Baker huddled, speaking in quiet tones. Then suddenly Mrs. Baker said, "Ah, all done. I'm sorry for any upset. Please accept my apology on your daughter's behalf".

"Thank you. I shall do", said Alice. She collected her shopping, signed the ledger and they said their good-byes, and Alice and Ethel left the shop, with the door bell ringing behind them.

"Well I never expected such a reaction", said Mrs. Baker to Mildred.

"Yes I know, or I think I do, but all is not well with that child, and I'm sure Graeme knows a little more about it than Lord Turner does, if you get my meaning?", said Mildred.

"I think we need to look into this ourselves", said Mrs. Baker, "Without the men for now. They seem to see things differently, for now".

"The child, Ethel", said Mildred quietly, "She seems to think that she is owed a gift from Graeme, but I can't find out why for now".

"And maybe you never will", said Mrs. Baker mysteriously.

"It's the egg she wants", said Mildred, "And the men, or Sam at least, say that Graeme is talking to it, and then Ethel reacts like that! What do you think Mrs. Baker?".

"I'll have to think it over", said Mrs. Baker, pulling a face, in thought.

As they stepped outside of the shop, Alice looked around. There was no sign of Sam anywhere. "Come along Ethel. Let's go straight home", said Alice.

Ethel appeared to be lost in thought, but listlessly nodded, and they both started to walk back, from whence they came.

Chapter seven

———•◆•———

S AM WAS CLEARING space in the barn, awaiting a new delivery, when Jimmy came into the barn looking for him. "Goodday Samuel", said Jimmy, tilting his cap, towards Sam.

"And a goodday to you as well Jimmy", replied Sam. "What can I do for you? If you don't mind me asking?".

"I was just speaking to one of the women passing by. There's a request from Mrs. Baker, for you to bring her an extra dozen eggs, if you'd be so kind, and she'll see to it that there's an extra pastry for you or your family for your trouble, seeing as how you've already made the trip once today", said Jimmy.

"Aye, I will do. Thank thee for bringing this to me Jimmy", said Sam.

"My pleasure", said Jimmy with a smile. Tweaked the peak of his cap, and wandered off.

Sam heaved a sigh. Moved one more bag of flour, left the barn, picked up the eggs from their resting place, just outside, and started to make his way back to the shop.

When he arrived, he opened the door to the tinkling of the bell and called out, "Goodday Mrs. Baker, I have brought a dozen eggs as was requested".

"I'll be there in a minute Sam. Don't leave just yet. I have to put them in my ledger", called back Mrs. Baker, who was nowhere to be seen.

Sam took the eggs over to the counter and set them down. A few moments later, Mrs. Baker entered through the doorway, behind the counter. "Goodday Sam", said Mrs. Baker.

"Goodday Mrs. Baker, twelve eggs as you requested", said Sam.

"Please put them down over there Sam", Mrs. Baker pointed to a place to her right and then said, "And I'd like a quick word about earlier, if you've the time or the mind to speak calmly and slowly to me. I've a few questions I'd like answered, that's all, and I'll answer a few for you, if you've a mind to ask".

"Aye, well, I've a mind to put these eggs over here, but I'll listen to what you say and speak only if I've a mind to do so", said Sam.

With that, Sam gently picked up the eggs and placed them where he'd been asked to do so, before returning to the counter. He stood there, arms crossed and looked Mrs. Baker squarely in the face.

"Now Sam, I don't want you to shout, but, do you remember that little girl from today, with Mildred and her mother?", asked Mrs. Baker.

"Yes, I do, as it happens", said Sam.

"She took a terrible fright, after you left the shop", said Mrs. Baker.

"How does that concern me Mrs. Baker?", asked Sam, slightly squinting his eyes to look more closely at Mrs. Baker.

"Well...., it does and it doesn't, you see Sam? If you know what I mean?", said Mrs. Baker.

Sam blew out a long breath, looked to his left, for no apparent reason, then swung his head, to once again, look directly into Mrs. Baker's face. Then he said, "I'm beginning to though, aren't I?".

"Well you might as well know, as you're one of the first to meet her, that Mildred and I, still nought to do with you though, have come to the conclusion, that somebody around here is giving that child a fright", said Mrs. Baker.

"And that concerns me, how?", said Sam sternly.

"I'd like your advice Sam, but no shouting please. Not at this time of day, or in my shop", said Mrs. Baker.

Sam sniffed up his left nostril, then said, "Maybe you should start at the beginning, if it in someway concerns me, and I'll correct thee if ye make a mistake".

"She screamed when I mentioned the Dale Ghoul", said Mrs. Baker boldly. Standing upright and straight faced.

"Oh don't gift me that. I never mentioned .....", started Sam, only to be interupted by Mrs. Baker, who said,

"Ok, Ok, Ok, I know that, but please hear me out. I've not finished the puzzle that's got us in a muddle".

"I still don't see what this is to me?", said Sam, growing irate.

"Oh please Sam, don't start. Not here. Not now. I want your help. Your input. I'm not here to put you in any trouble", said Mrs. Baker. Mildly cowering behind the counter.

"Is there anybody else here?", asked Sam.

"No. There certainly is not", said Mrs. Baker.

"Anyone peeking or spying from behind your doorway, per chance?", said Sam.

"Oh Sam, what a thing to say. I've known you all these years and never once have I set you up for any crime, or dinner, or punishment, either", said Mrs. Baker sternly.

"Aye, well, go on then", said Sam. "What else is new to you, that you want me to know about".

"Well, truth of the matter is, we wonder where she found out or heard about the curse", said Mrs. Baker.

"Well why don't you ask her?", asked Sam bluntly.

"She won't speak", said Mrs. Baker.

"What did you say to her?", asked Sam.

"I've never said a word, except what you heard. I mentioned the Dale Ghoul. Said it might be an ancient God, a devil or a spirit, and she screamed. Wouldn't speak ...... Her mother had to take her out of the shop. Post-haste", said Mrs. Baker.

"So?", said Sam inquisitively.

"Mildred says she's after Graeme's egg. The golden egg, that you say holds his wife's memories", said Mrs. Baker earnestly.

"So what? I still don't see what this is to me?", said Sam.

"Well that's why I was speaking about the golden egg that Graeme holds", said Mrs. Baker.

"What has the golden egg that Graeme holds, got to do with the Dale Ghoul? If you don't mind me asking, that is?", said Sam.

"All I said, was that you believe, or say you heard, that it's his wife's memories that he speaks to. I only said I believed or had heard, it was the Dale Ghoul that talked to him from the golden egg", said Mrs. Baker, tight-lipped.

"Why did you say that to her?", asked Sam.

"You started it Sam. I asked you, what did you hear about Graeme, and you told me of the golden egg. What were you possibly thinking?", asked Mrs. Baker.

"That's all I know of him", said Sam. "So that's all I said. Why did you ask me?", asked Sam.

"Ooh Sam! You've caused such an upset. Somebody is upsetting this child. You're talking of golden eggs instead of people. The child is asking about curses and screaming, at the mentioning of a ghoul, and there's witches in the area, that you know about, but can't remember who told you about them, or what they're doing here. What was Graeme's wife to you? Why are you bothered about where she was buried .... ?", said Mrs. Baker.

"Hang on! Hang on a moment!", interrupted Sam.

"Oh no, not until I've finished ...... , or who do you know who's bothered by it? And what's the connection with these witches, that either have been here, or are coming here? In relation to what you seem to regard as an ongoing feud or oddity over Graeme's wife's death", said Mrs. Baker.

"Ah!", started Sam.

"No! Not yet! This is still my shop. Don't you forget that, and I want the full and complete truth out of you. No matter what it takes. Do you hear me Samuel Jones?", said Mrs. Baker, quite irately now.

"I had nought to do with them witches, Mrs. Baker. Honestly it's true", said Sam.

"Not like that Samuel Jones. You can comeback when you have a complete and full answer for me", said Mrs. Baker.

"Oh not again", said Sam, as he took his cap off. Turned and walked out the door, to the tinkling of the bell.

Mildred ran out of the door, behind Mrs. Baker in excitement.

"That showed him, eh? He won't be quite so brutish next time he comes here. I can tell you that for nought, Mildred", said Mrs. Baker.

"Do you think he'll mind helping our inquiry like this?", asked Mildred.

"Oh, he'll be fine. They're simple enough questions for a man with his mind. Come on, I'll put the kettle on. The leisure club gets answers out of the likes of him in no time at all", said Mrs. Baker.

After Alice and Ethel had passed the cottages, Ethel asked, "Am I a ghost, a ghoul, a spirit or a devil?", of Alice, without looking at her, before adding, "For your Ethel's sake, not mine. For I feel safe now. No-one can tell us apart, as yet".

Alice sighed. "I'm not sure dear Ethel, but I know you're no devil. You're far too polite, but please, don't scream when people talk of such things. It really gives everybody a terrible fright, in my opinion", replied Alice.

They neared the bend in the road. Ethel began to jump up and look over the hedge.

"What are you looking at?", asked Alice.

"Turner's pond, oh Turner's pond. There must be a story about Turner's pond", said Ethel.

"Really?", laughed Alice, but Ethel continued,

"Oh tell me, oh tell me, or find out the truth. Tell me why Turner's pond is disused".

"I'll see what I can do for you", said Alice, before she continued, "It's nearly lunchtime, but we still may see someone on our way home, with whom we can discuss Turner's pond".

"Oh goody, oh goody, oh goody, and my egg? Oh when can I have my egg and my home?", asked Ethel, lightly skipping in front of Alice, and looking back at her, from time to time.

"Oh Ethel, it's not yours yet. You shouldn't talk like that", said Alice, with a smile.

"But I want, but I want, but I want, do I, the golden egg that looks like a ball", said Ethel.

"I'll try to get it for you once more", replied Alice.

"Only once?", said Ethel sternly, coming to a standstill and staring at Alice.

"Today that is", said Alice, as Ethel whooped for joy, and continued to skip, "I did promise, after all", finished Alice, with a wry smile.

Chapter eight

———•◆•———

SAM WALKED DEJECTEDLY back to the mill, thinking, 'What did I think of Graeme's wife? Of Graeme? What did I hear? And what did I see? Who told me? Come on man, think! Answer me!'.

As he got to the mill, he was greeted by Jimmy. "All done then?", asked Jimmy of Sam.

"Aye! I'm all done for now thanks to thee", said Sam grumpily.

"Oh, it didn't go well then? Taking all those eggs up to the shop then?", said Jimmy.

"No it didn't. That flippin' Mrs. Baker has started her own investigation into these witch-sightings", said Sam.

"I'd stay out of that, if I were you. You don't want all that clackety-clack, going on inside your mind, now do you?", said Jimmy.

"Too late. I'm deemed the star witness for now", said Sam.

"You'd better go home. Lie down and take some rest", said Jimmy.

"I'll be all right. I'll carry on with my duties for now. My mother will go mad, if she finds out, I'm involved with the Leisure Club again", said Sam.

"On your own head be it then. Who is it this time?", asked Jimmy.

"Graeme again, and his deceased wife again, and his Lordship's flamin' new bosses wife and child. That's who it is, this flippin' time. I'll tell ye....", started Sam irately.

"Ah! Ah! Ah! You'll no be taking me down the road with ye now. Talkin' like that about his Lordship. What you need to do, seeing as how you'll no take my advice, is get back into the barn, work as quickly as you can, and hopefully you'll be finished before the day is out, moving all that stuff about", said Jimmy.

"Aye, that I will", said Sam, who trudged off, back to the barn, and then started trying to remember what he was doing, what needed to be moved and where did it need moving to.

Jimmy shook his head sadly, watching Sam for a moment or two, as he worked, and then returned back to the main office building.

As he walked through, one of the typists asked Jimmy to report to Eric's office. Jimmy made his way up the stairs, knocked on Eric's door, and awaited a reply.

Eric opened the door, "Ah Jimmy, just the man. Come in, come in. Master Guild is calling later, on a matter of business, and I want a full update as to what is going on". Jimmy entered Eric's office and stood before Eric's desk, as Eric closed the door and retook his seat.

Jimmy quickly took off his cap, and held it in both hands, in front of him. "Well, go on. What's happening that's new, that I don't know about?", demanded Eric, leaning forward. Picking up a pencil, and pointing it at Jimmy.

"I don't know what you mean, Mr. Marshall", replied Jimmy.

"Well, let's start with Eric shall we. He was seen leaving the yard, after speaking almost directly to you, by someone looking out of the main building's window. Can you describe or explain that to me, eh?", asked Eric, who then tapped the table with his pencil, and then leaned back in his chair, as Jimmy gulped. As he, himself, awaited Jimmy's answer.

"Well man, don't just stand there. Answer me! What did you say to him? Did you know where he went and how long was he away from his duties for?", he demanded again.

Still no answer, as Jimmy began to look around the office. Eric was about to speak again, when suddenly Jimmy looked straight at him and said, "Please sir! It's not like that. I was asked to send him to Mrs. Baker".

"Really?", said Eric, who once again leaned back into his chair and then said, "And who was this by? then, eh? Who is running this yard nowadays? And why was he asked to go there again, when he had already been earlier today? .... And I want the truth out of you. None of this Tomfoolery, that you folks around here are so fond off, according to Lord Turner".

"It's not like that", said Jimmy nervously, looking down at his cap, and then mumbling, "It was one of the passing women".

"Speak up man! I can't hear you. Look at me again, and tell me loudly and clearly", snapped Eric.

Jimmy gulped, looked up at Eric, who was staring at him, fiercely in the face, and said again, "It was one of the local women passing by, that's all".

"And who put her in charge of you and Sam? If I might be so bold as to ask you?", asked Eric, mildly gentler this time.

"Mrs. Baker did, that's all", said Jimmy, as his head fell down again.

"Why did you not", started Eric, then, "Look at me Jimmy! For goodness sake. Why did you not come upstairs and ask me? Instead of sending him out looking like a thief, with a bundle of eggs in his hand, eh? Can you tell me that?", asked Eric.

"I .....", began Jimmy, who gulped, and then continued, "I was asked not to bother you".

"Who by?", asked Eric.

No reply.

So Eric pushed on, "This woman, local or not". Jimmy looked up quickly towards Eric, at that. "Did she put you up to this, eh? Was it her? Have you ever seen her before in the area, or did you just presume she was a local?", asked Eric firmly.

"I", gulped Jimmy again, who then looked back at the floor.

"Well?", asked Eric more mildly.

"It's just that she said it would be all right, and it would only take a minute or two of his time, and no. I did not recognise her", said Jimmy.

"I hope you're not lying to me. I will have Mrs. Baker's ledger checked for the delivery", said Eric, as he pulled a mean face, looked slowly around his office, then back at Jimmy and said, "I personally saw him return. I'm not saying I'll have his wages docked, not if Mrs. Baker's ledger is correct, nor will I inform the police. For it will all be present and correct, but, I insist, for this to happen, that you tell me what was said between you both, on his return. Remembering I want no lies, word for word if you can, and I saw how long you were speaking to each other for", said Eric sternly, wagging his finger slowly in warning towards Jimmy.

"I .....", said Jimmy again, then, "Oh, all right. He said Mrs. Baker is looking into the witches on his Lordship's behalf, and he is helping her".

"Is he now?", asked Eric.

"Well, he said he is", said Jimmy.

"What else did he say?", asked Eric.

"Seems to think, in my opinion, not that it's any of my business, but that there are questions being asked about a Mr. Daniels from the post-office, and your wife and child, that's all", said Jimmy quickly, who then started to look at his cap again, which he began turning in his hands.

"My wife?", asked Eric.

"Yes sir, but that's all I know. I'll no take part in any witch-hunt, or investigation. Honestly, he's the one you need to ask, not me. I never spoke to Mrs. Baker. Honestly! It's true", said Jimmy in panic.

71

Eric eased back into his chair. "Aye! I think I believe you. Find Mildred if you can. I'd like to have a word with her. Preferably before Mr. Guild arrives. Oh, and one last thing. What did you say to him?", asked Eric thoughtfully.

"Oh Mr. Marshall, it weren't like that. I did suggest he go home and lie down for a while, but I never said, but I did expect him to speak to you about it before he left, but it was only because he said he never felt well, but he never said why, and I only said so out of kindness, but he decided to return to work, and said he'd be fine, but I wasn't trying to get him or me into any trouble at the time, and I was becoming concerned of the way he was speaking about witches, and his Lordship's investigation into it", said Jimmy.

"What about his Lordship's investigation into it? The witchcraft, I mean?", asked Eric.

"I don't know about these witches. I've not seen them. All I know is that 'is Lordship is looking into it, and I've enough on my plate with my wife and family, and other duties, for me not to be involved in his investigation into them", said Jimmy.

"You're not telling me the full truth, are you?", asked Eric.

"Oh please sir, I'm scared of witches and witchcraft, there's nothing else I can tell you with any truth in it", said Jimmy. "Please, don't send me mad, just for passing a message on".

"Oh, all right", said Eric, "But it might not be the last you hear of this. Find Mildred, get her to come here, any way that you can. The sooner the better, and not just for me, but for you too now, as well", he threatened.

"Yes sir, straight away sir", said Jimmy.

"Go on, out you go", said Eric, waving his hand towards the door.

Jimmy turned and left. As he shut the office door behind him, he was confronted by a group of laughing and smiling typists. "Go Jimmy. Go and do thy master's bidding", one of them said, laughingly. "I can't wait to tell your wife and children about this".

Jimmy stood up bold, put his cap firmly upon his head, and said, "Needs must, ladies! Please excuse me", and with that, he marched boldly past the tittering women.

Chapter nine

———•◦•———

ALICE AND ETHEL passed Turner's pond, went past the Welsh's cottage and began to approach Graeme's cottage.

"Is he there?", asked Ethel of Alice, as quietly as she dared, but still to be heard.

"I'm not sure", replied Alice, beginning to stare. "He may have gone inside for his lunch or a drink, or even to rest or lie-down". She looked harder, but then had to admit, "I can't see him at all in his garden".

"Shall we knock at his door?", asked Ethel excitedly.

Alice smiled, and nearly laughed out loud. "We can't do that. It's not deemed fitting", said Alice.

"Why not? Why not? Oh what is this riddle of fitting?", said Ethel.

"We have no reason to call, and people may talk, and wonder, why? Oh why, did we call?", said Alice with a pained smile. "Hush now! We are nearly there". They walked on in silence.

As they drew level with the cottage, they saw Graeme working on one of his windows, to the north side of his cottage. "Goodday to you again Master Graeme", said Alice.

Graeme looked up in shock. "Goodday to you both again", said Graeme, as he put down his tools and walked towards them, saying, "But I'll no be a Master to you both, not today, for I'm still well enough not to need a maid. Today at least, and for now, I can say".

"I'd like to ask thee again, since Mildred's not around to intervene, if you've a mind to sell Ethel your egg, or your home, because she, as in Ethel, keeps asking me for it", said Alice.

"Oh my!", exclaimed Graeme. "I'll try to explain. Listen up Ethel".

Graeme stopped just behind his hedgerow, and looked up to the sky in a ponderous way, then said, "Once upon a time, Ethel, I had great hopes and dreams, with this wife of mine. Now departed into another realm, but I found and I find that I miss her.

"Like you, or similar to you, I find that I recall my past hopes and dreams, when I see this gift that was for us. I and some others, call it a gift with some sentimental value, because it recalls the happy times that we spent together.

"I can no give up this gift, nor as yet, let the memories move on. So I have to say, 'no I cannot sell you my golden egg'. Please do not ask me, or another, or your mother, for me to sell you my golden egg. Do you understand me, Ethel?".

"Yes", replied Ethel, who then continued, "I'll not ask thee or another, for you to sell me your egg, but you may want to move on one day, and when you do, please remember you can gift me your egg, almost anytime that you like".

"Thank you. I will remember your words, as you remember mine", said Graeme.

"Thank you Graeme, for your time, to speak to Ethel", said Alice. "We'll be on our way home to get some lunch and to put our shopping away", she finished.

"Yes well, have a goodday, to you both again. I'll be stopping for lunch myself, when I've finished repairing my shutter", replied Graeme.

"What do you know of Turner's pond?", asked Ethel, halting both Alice and Graeme from moving on. "Mr. Daniels, please, do you have time to explain?", she continued, with a smile and a small courtesy.

Graeme looked to Alice, who looked back, and shrugged. "Well!", he started to say, shaking his head slowly, from side to side.

"We would like to know. It seems dis-used", said Alice with an encouraging look and a nod of her head.

"Aye, it is", said Graeme. "With good cause too, in my opinion, for what it's worth".

"Is it cursed?", asked Ethel sternly.

"Oh good grief! No! It certainly isn't, but they do say it's haunted by a ghost, those that know about such things, that is to say", said Graeme.

"Oh please do say. It may shed some light upon the witches in the area", said Alice, with a tight-lipped smile. Feeling, rather than seeing, a stare from Ethel.

Graeme laughed briefly, then said, "Aye, that it might, but it was a while back. Way before I was born, some hundreds of years ago".

"Oh go on. Tell us more. If you can or you like to", said Alice encouragingly.

Graeme noticed both, Alice and Ethel, looking at him, as a captive audience, and decided, "Oh all right. I'll tell thee what I know".

"I'm glad about that. I'll be questioned about it from now till goodness knows when, if you don't", said Alice with an encouraging smile.

"Well", said Graeme, rubbing his chin, then continuing, "A few hundred years back, during the witch-hunts, the Lords came from way over t'other side of the county, with soldiers to boot. They came through the village. It was quite different than it is today, mind you.

"Looking for people who would not change their religion, to the new belief. Most folks gave in, but one woman, very unpopular she was, refused. So they put her to trial".

He pursed his lips, looked around at the hills. and then back to his audience. Lowering his voice and his tone, he continued, "Lots of folks had complaints about her, but she wouldn't admit to the crimes, so they put her in the stocks for three days and three nights, on the village green. The villagers back then, they all threw rotten vegetables and eggs at her. Spat at her, and some even kicked or hit her, or both, but still she wouldn't admit to any witchcraft".

"Oh what did they do?", asked Alice, intriguedly.

"What's that to do with the pond?", asked Ethel, alarmed.

"Aye, well, I were coming to that", said Graeme, taking a pace or two, and looking up and down the road this time, before saying, "What they did, they built a huge bonfire, with a stake in the middle of it. Then the Lord declared ….".

Graeme stood back, lifted his head up, and stretched both of his arms outwards. "Hear ye! All of ye. There is but one test for a witch", he said quite loudly, and then, "We shall duck her into the pond three times. If she survives, then we shall know she is a witch, for witches do not drown".

Then Graeme dropped his head, and pointed at Alice and Ethel. Lowered his voice once again, and said, "And if she is a witch, we will burn her at the stake".

Graeme relaxed at this. Smiled and stood normally for a few moments, before saying, "The villagers were delighted. So they tied a chair onto a large pole. Took it, and the witch, down to Turner's pond, shackled she were, but still they taunted her, and threw stones and vegetables at her.

"When they got her to the pond. They tied her to the chair, and ducked her in the pond, for as long as they dared. Asking each time for a confession, of her witchcraft. Regrettably though, she died. She was not a witch at all. They were ever so disappointed. They'd even built the bonfire to burn her", he said sadly.

"Oh that's terribly sad", said Alice.

"Why is it haunted though?", asked Ethel.

Alice stared at Ethel. Graeme chuckled again and then said, "Aye, well, some folks say, they see movement down there at night, and hear her screams, because her soul don't rest easy. For she was proven not to be a witch, because she drowned, and they just left her body there, in the pond".

"Why did they do that? Mr. Daniels, if I may be so bold as to ask?", questioned Alice.

"Well, they went after their other suspects, three women and one man. One of them confessed whilst being tortured, and all four of them got burnt at the stake, the same day as the confession took place", he said proudly.

"But the ghost?", asked Ethel.

"Oh, she was not a Christian, so everybody decided not to bury her in the cemetery, just in case she came back to haunt them", said Graeme.

"What of the Dale Ghoul? What do you know of that?", asked Ethel, suddenly confused.

"Well, some call it that, for the ghost would go up to the farm, because it's believed she worked there, see?", asked Graeme.

"The farm......", started Ethel agog.

"Is this a joke to scare Ethel? Or can you tell me who told you this, Mr. Daniels?", said Alice.

"It's as I was told it, when I was a child, way younger than young Ethel, here, but, so I'm told, these sightings of movement and strange sounds at night, are the very reason why nobody, not even the Lord or Master, would trouble to use the pond, at day or night, if you take my meaning", said Graeme, with a grimace.

"What's the Dale ghoul like, Mr. Daniels?", asked Ethel.

"Eh?", asked Graeme.

"Do you ever speak to her, I mean, at night?", asked Ethel.

Graeme looked at Alice. Alice smiled tight-lippedly, and then said, "I think it's because you live near the pond".

"Oh good grief! No", said Graeme, and then he added, "I would never knowingly conspire with a witch".

"But she's not a witch Graeme, she was innocent, so you said", added Alice.

"Oh! Yes, so she was. Witches are spooking me at the moment though", admitted Graeme.

"Oh that's Ok, I'll think on what you've said", said Alice. Then she noticed Ethel, staring back down the road from whence they came, towards Turner's pond. "I'd better take Ethel home. I think she must be hungry", she finished.

"Ah yes, I've work to get done myself, before I stop for lunch. Have a safe journey home, to you both", finished Graeme.

They parted with a few farewells. Graeme returned to his window shutter repairing, and Alice and Ethel set of up the road in silence.

Chapter ten

———•◆•———

As TIME PASSED, Eric looked around his office. His desk, though large, was usually cluttered with papers. These were cleared away now and placed on shelves and in drawers, around the sides of, in his opinion, his small office, as he awaited Master Guild, from Guild's farm.

He had a chair ready for Master Guild. It would be his first meeting with Master Guild, the local farmer. A chance to impress him, with his managerial skills and negotiating prowess.

He straightened up his tie, looked out of his window again, hoping to see him arrive in the yard, whilst wondering if there was anything that he'd missed about the operations at the mill.

He knew where he had placed his records, should he need them. He knew the prices he bought and sold at. Suddenly, there was a knock at the door.

"Who is it?", called out Eric, in mild surprise.

"It's me, Mildred", came back the reply.

Eric went to the door and saw Mildred on the other side. "Oh please, come in Mildred", he said, opening the door widely and gesturing with his left arm.

"Thank you", said Mildred, who entered the office.

Eric closed the door and returned to his seat.

"Jimmy said you would like to see me urgently", said Mildred, "Is that correct?".

"Oh yes", interjected Eric. "A matter of importance has come up. Master Guild is arriving this afternoon for a meeting. I need to be in the knowledge of all that is going on hereabouts", he concluded.

"How does that concern me?", asked Mildred.

"I have heard Mrs. Baker has started a witch-hunt. What do you know about it?", asked Eric.

"Nothing!", admitted Mildred.

"Then why was Sam sent back to the shop today? What do you know about it? And what is the involvement of my wife and daughter, in this matter?", asked Eric.

"Sam delivered some extra eggs. I arrived there, just as he left", said Mildred.

"Did he see you?", queried Eric.

"Not that I`m aware of", said Mildred.

"Ok, carry on", said Eric.

"Mrs. Baker and I are looking into an incident involving Ethel, your daughter", said Mildred.

"Really? And just what is this incident? If I may be so bold as to ask, about my own daughter? Why was I not informed earlier? And what business is it of yours and Mrs. Baker`s?", demanded Eric.

"Ethel got upset at the mention of the Dale ghoul", said Mildred.

"Go on! I'm all ears", he prompted her, leaning back in his chair. "You can tell me about the Dale ghoul later".

"She screamed in Mrs. Baker's shop. Mrs. Baker, Alice, Ethel and myself had just been speaking a little earlier, to Graeme Daniels", said Mildred, who then added, "I was going to inform you about it, when I saw you next, and as it's Mrs. Baker's shop, she wanted it looking into immediately".

"This Dale ghoul, what is it? Why was it mentioned? And why did it make Ethel scream?", asked Eric.

"In my opinion, but I am a Christian, it's nothing but folklore, but, Mrs. Baker said it may be an ancient God, a devil or a spirit, in her opinion, or so she has been told. It was mentioned, going back to why Mrs. Baker wanted to speak with Sam, because Sam was speaking about Graeme, when he was there", said Mildred.

"Do you mean to say, you were all gossiping?", queried Eric.

"Well, Alice and I were interested in finding out a little of Graeme, due to his age, and the possibility of him employing a maid in his old age", said Mildred.

"Alice?", asked Eric.

"Well, she never spoke, that's true, but there are rumours about Graeme and that's as far as our investigation has got", said Mildred.

"Why did it's mention cause Ethel to scream,?", asked Eric.

"I don't know. Alice calmed Ethel down, and they left almost straight away", said Mildred.

"Almost?", queried Eric, leaning forward in his chair again.

"Well, Alice got to sign the ledger and collected her shopping, and they departed", said Mildred.

Eric sat back in his chair and thought for a few moments. "Ok, keep me informed as to why it was mentioned for now. That will be all for now Mildred", he finished.

"Thank you Mr. Marshall. I shall do", finished Mildred, who smiled sweetly and left the room, to a cheer from downstairs.

Eric looked up in surprise, then heard Mildred say, "Oh, goodday to you Master Guild, it is an honour to meet you again".

Eric jumped up, out of seat, as he heard a gruff voice say, "Goodday to you Mildred. I hope all is well with you and your family".

"Yes thank you Master Guild. I must be on my way though, for I have much to do today", said Mildred.

Just then, a portly man, slightly balding, appeared in Eric's doorway. Facing to the right and saying, "Good-bye my dear".

"Good-bye Master Guild", Eric heard Mildred sing.

The man turned towards Eric, dressed in black tailor-made trousers, a red waist-coat and a white shirt.

He checked his pocket-watch, turned to face Eric, and then said, "And who might you be sir?".

Eric gulped, and said, "Why? I'm, Mr. Marshall. The new manager Eric Marshall actually".

He could hear the sound of laughing, from the typists outside.

"Oh don't worry about them tittering women. I have an appointment with thee, and I be, Master Guild. Are you going to invite me into your poky office for a chat then, or what?", said Master Guild.

"Please come in and take a seat Master Guild. Would you like any refreshment?", asked Eric.

"A cup of tea and some of Mrs. Baker's pastries, would be nice", said Master Guild.

Eric stuck his head out of his office door. "Some tea and pastries for Master Guild and myself", he said.

All the women in the typing pool laughed.

"Never mind them Marshall. Come! Sit down! Remember I'll no be a part of your investigation team", said Master Guild.

Eric returned to his seat. "Now then, there's a few rules you need to know before we start, but you can close your door if you've a mind to", said Master Guild.

Eric rose from his seat, closed the office door and re-seated himself. "And what are they, Master Guild?", he asked.

"You don't bother me with your questions, got it?", asked Master Guild, eyeing Eric with one eye.

"Yes, got that one", said Eric.

"You also don't bother any of my workers, past or present, with your questions, got it?", asked Master Guild.

"But my orders are very clear Master Guild. I must know exactly what is going on at the mill. Lord Turner insists it is to be so", said Eric resolutely.

"Lord Turner's business is Lord Turner's business. Guild's farm business and it's workers are my business. If you have any unsurmountable problem with any of my workers, whether they be here or not, because I do send my employees here from time to time and I expect them to return in one piece, all of them, then you can send your Lord Turner around, or turn up with the police and make a formal complaint, but that is the protection, I as one of the mills major suppliers, offer to my employees", said Master Guild.

"Yes sir", said Eric.

There was a knock at the door. "Come dear", called out Master Guild. In walked one of the young typists, carrying a tray, with the makings of tea and a plate of Mrs. Baker's pastries.

"Here you are Master Guild", she said, leaning over him to place the tray down, and then turning to give him a big smile.

"Just the way you like it", she finished, with a sexy smile.

Master Guild laughed, slapped her on the behind, and grabbed a handful of her rump.

"Ooh Master Guild. I hope your wife never finds out", she teased.

"And woe be`tied any person who ever tells her, you little floozy. Go on, out you go", said Master Guild. Then to Eric he said, "That's how you should treat them Eric. Horsewhip and flog them, if they don't do as they're told. Same with the men. You included by the way, just so you know whose side I'm on".

The young woman stood in the doorway for a moment or two. Winked at Eric when she saw him look at her, and then closed the door behind her, quietly.

"I expect all the women around here, to still be working here, next time I'm around. From Mildred to that young typist, and Mrs. Baker too", said Master Guild, as he picked up a pastry and stuffed half of it into his mouth and began to chew.

Eric sat there in silence.

When Master Guild swallowed, he continued, "She makes wonderful pastries, does Mrs. Baker. I'm sure Alice does too".

"She does occasionally", agreed Eric.

"Ah, that's good, but I don't like falling out with any of the local lasses, because they treat me right, and you don't want to fall out with me, because your job, or the mill might collapse, and that means you have to bend your rules for me, just a little, if we are to do business. If you take my meaning Eric? I can call you Eric, can't I?", asked Master Guild.

"Yes you can call me Eric", declared Eric, as he sat and watched Master Guild continue to eat his pastry.

After a short while, Eric added, "I will try to cooperate the best I can".

Master Guild spat some of the pastry out onto the table, "What?", he exclaimed loudly.

The office door opened. The young typist stuck her head in, "Are you all right Master Guild? Can I get you anything?".

She walked in to survey the damage.

"Do I have any crumbs on me, my dear?", asked Master Guild.

"Oh let me look", she said.

She walked seductively over to Master Guild, and began to run her hands gently over his chest. "There's a few crumbs here, but I'll get them off for you now", she said.

"Ah, so you see Eric, this is how business gets done around here. I think you'd better do more than try to cooperate, or you might find yourself on your way somewhere new", said Master Guild.

The young typist turned from her work, smiled at Eric, and then pulled tongues at him.

"If you see what I mean Eric? Go on wench, I'll sort you out later", said Master Guild, as the young woman turned and smiled at Master Guild. Gave him a hug, then went to leave, but stopped suddenly, only to whisper into Master Guild's ear.

She then turned to smile, at Eric. Laughed at him and then ran out of the room and closed the door.

Eric felt restraint, then said, "Are there any other rules I need to know Master Guild?".

"None for now. I'll tell you when they change, but for now, I want to discuss business with you. Too see what kind of a manager Lord Turner has found himself, since the last one passed away", said Master Guild.

"And what business would you like to discuss, then?", asked Eric.

"Well now, I would like to keep profits at a maximum. I've seen a window of opportunity. I want your help on the matter, but, you'll need to convince Lord Turner it's a good deal", said Master Guild.

"What opportunity would that be then?", asked Eric.

"I can reduce my workforce by one. I can cut my wages bill. Do you understand that?", asked Master Guild.

"Yes I do, but how does that involve me?", asked Eric.

"I have a few concerns locally, business concerns that is. I make deliveries to many local towns, such as Daleville town. The supplier to Daleville town, lives the other side of Isop hill. He has to send a special delivery to Daleville town. We were speaking at the Hunter's Lodge last month ,when we realised we had virtually the same shipment. This farmer and I want to swap deliveries. I'll need one less deliverer and he gets more work from his deliverers, because they can save themselves over half a day, a trip", said Master Guild, who then began to slurp his tea.

"I can see how that can save you money", admitted Eric.

There was a knock at the door.

"Come in", said Master Guild.

The young typist entered, "Will that be all, or can I get you anything else Master Guild", she said.

"Oh that's all for now my dear. Please don't knock next time I'm here", Master Guild said.

"Thank you Master Guild", said the young typist, closing the door behind her.

Eric sat thoughtfully for a few moments, then said, "How can I be of any help in this matter?".

"Ah, my good man. I'm glad you asked. How about I introduce, next month at the Lodge, you to this farmer friend of mine. He'll be able to explain his part in this, and then we'll leave it up to you, to sort it out with Lord Turner. He'll be ever so pleased, this farmer friend of mine, that you've agreed to discuss this with him", said Master Guild.

He then stood up, and began to walk to the door, "I'll send Mildred over with the exact date of the meeting", he finished.

"Mildred?", queried Eric.

"Yes Mildred. She often comes over with news. I know her well. I like to deal with people I know. It's why I feel comfortable working with women I know, if you know what I mean?", said Master Guild.

"Yes", stammered Eric, "I.....".

Suddenly, the door got opened by the young typist, who gestured Master Guild out of the room.

Eric followed, leaving his sentence unfinished.

All the typists burst out laughing, when they saw Eric's expression, as he looked towards Master Guild.

"You look after all of my girls Eric. Maybe I'll find a job for your wife at the farm, or in the shop", said Master Guild.

"Ooh, that will be nice", called out the typists.

"I don't know about that. I'll have to speak to her about it", replied Eric.

"Yes....., well, it can't be doing her good, stuck in your home all day, with you at work and no company, but your daughter. She must be terribly lonely", said Master Guild.

The workers downstairs cheered and the women typists laughed, as Master Guild continued, "So you can let me know, next month at the Lodge. It will give you something to talk about", whilst giving Eric a meaningful look. Then he added, "It must be wonderful to work in such a happy workplace. I always look forward to my visits here".

Again there was a cheer from downstairs, as Master Guild began to descend the stairs, and the smiling women returned to their work. Eric grimaced, and then returned to his office, hearing the tinkling of tittering from the typing pool, as he closed the door behind him.

Chapter eleven

As THEY REACHED the end of the road, both Alice and Ethel looked right, towards the main part of the village, but turned left, to return to their home. There were no people outside the two cottages on their right and the sun shone brightly above Craggy Tor, upon their left.

Ethel looked at Alice, and broke the silence by saying, "This Ghoul ......, has it become me?".

"No Ethel. You shouldn't think like that. You should think of the egg", said Alice.

"The egg?", asked Ethel quickly.

"Yes the egg. The big golden egg that is Graeme's. That's where the Ghoul lives", said Alice, with a smile.

"Yes", said Ethel, looking at the top of the peak of Graggy Tor, and then saying, after a few moments, "Yes, you're right. I must have the egg. It will prove it's not me".

"Oh Ethel!", exclaimed Alice, with a sidelong glance.

"But I want it! But I want it! But I want it, I do!", Ethel expletively and sulkily exclaimed.

"Really?", asked Alice, quite callously.

"Yes really", said Ethel, then, "I want it no matter what, I want! I want it no matter what".

Alice replied, "Ok, to keep thee happy, as he will not sell, I'll get it for you within twenty years".

"Why so long?", asked Ethel, confused again.

"As he will not sell and its wrong to steal, I will lead him to the belief, he should gift it to you for free", said Alice.

"Yippee!", exclaimed Ethel, then excitedly, "I love receiving a gift for free".

"Yes I know. That is why we do not steal, or harm our friends or loved ones", said Alice with a smile.

"But he's no friend of mine", said Ethel almost heatedly.

"Yes I know, but he will be, if he gifts you a golden ball or egg, maybe?", said Alice, almost playfully.

Ethel began to laugh "He-he", and skipped off, in front of Alice once more.

As Master Guild left the mill, Mildred found Jimmy in the yard, "Goodday to you Jimmy", said Mildred.

"Goodday Mildred, and how are you today?", asked Jimmy.

"I'm fine thank you. How is the family?", asked Mildred.

Jimmy gulped. "Well the lad's doing fine, and the little 'un is getting ready for school. The wife's awful busy", said Jimmy quickly.

"Ah, I remember the birth of your last born. Such a joyous occasion", said Mildred.

"Oh aye, the wife were awful pleased you where there to help her through it, as am I, and that we're all well and fit, and not homeless and poor", said Jimmy.

"Yes, well, in gratitude for my help, on that special day. I need your help, and whoever you can muster in support, whilst we try and soften Graeme up, to talk about his past", said Mildred.

"That's not fair Miss Mildred. We're a very poor family", said Jimmy, "With very few friends in the area".

"That's as maybe, but Eric wants, or rather Mr. Marshall, is interested in Graeme's latest involvement in Mrs. Baker's shop. I'd like for you to take personal charge and speak to Mr. Daniel's, in passing, and try to find out what goes on with this egg he holds", said Mildred.

"It will help Mrs. Baker, because there was an incident at the shop, only today, when it was mentioned. I need him thinking about it, fresh in the mind, that's all I'd like you to do for now. Take some friends along for support. Go to the inn if you like", she finished.

"The inn, Miss. Mildred? But the wife can be so unkind when I drink", said Jimmy.

"I'll speak to your wife, on your behalf. I mean, I did deliver your last child at your own request", said Mildred.

"And the wife's, that's true", said Jimmy.

"So you say, but, you don't want to take Mrs. Baker on, in a feud, do you now?", said Mildred.

"No! Not at all", said Jimmy, resolutely.

"Then take Sam along, and a few others, if you can, and take a drink or two. It may even cheer Sam up. He's looking ever so glum. Will you do that small thing for me? Jimmy? Eh?", asked Mildred.

"Aye, I will do, but, I, personally want no trouble, but I'll try to help Sam the best I can, so I'll see if I can get him to meet Graeme for thee", said Jimmy resignedly.

"Thank you Jimmy", said Mildred as she waved dismissively to Jimmy, and then returned to the main building, leaving Jimmy alone in the yard.

A few days later, Mildred left Eric's office, with her orders for the day. She started to make her way to the stairs, when one of the women typists said, "Mildred, Jimmy can go to the inn tomorrow, straight from work, with Sam and a couple of labourers from the mill floor", quietly.

"Thank you", said Mildrid, who started to descend the stairs.

As she reached the bottom, a passing labourer said, "Will Graeme be there? I wonder".

Another, closeby said, "He will be, if someone can keep him chatting in his garden".

Mildred looked around. The labourers passed on by. She marched resolutely across the work floor, and out, into the yard, only to be confronted by Jimmy.

"Have you cleared my way to take young Sam for a drink, by speaking to my wife yet?", asked Jimmy. "It seems to be driving everybody insane. It's all everybody's talking about, round here", he added, gesturing around the yard.

"I'll do it today, but I'll let you know tomorrow", she said with a smile.

"Aye, well, don't leave it too late. People have to let others know. I do know you know that, because you expect it yourself", said Jimmy.

"I'll let you know before I do my deliveries tomorrow. I have much to do. People to see, Deliveries to be made. Please, excuse me Jimmy, but I must rush if I am to do all I intend to do today", said Mildred.

"Aye, well, I hope you do, because I've still things to arrange myself, tomorrow", said Jimmy.

"Be sure of it then, even if I have to find you myself, or send Mrs. Baker looking for you, you'll know before I start my delivery round tomorrow", said Mildred.

"Goodday to you then", said Jimmy. "I'll no be slowing you down, when you've so much to do".

"Goodday to you also Jimmy", said Mildred, with a strained smile.

She collected her basket, filled it with some ground wheat, and set out to Mrs. Baker's shop.

She entered to the tinkling of a bell. Mrs. Baker, unusually, sat behind the counter instead of in her back room.

"Good morning Mrs. Baker", said Mildred.

"I've been waiting for you", said Mrs. Baker, half-closing one eye.

"I've too much to do, but I've brought some wheat. Do you have my deliveries ready?", asked Mildred.

"I do", said Mrs. Baker, unusually so, "There. Over there". She pointed with her pencil, into the corner, behind the door.

This surprised Mildred.

"All you have to do", said Mrs. Baker, "Is empty the wheat into that container, there". Mrs. Baker pointed to the other side of the door.

Mildred walked over and poured the ground wheat into the container. Then Mrs. Baker said, "And then collect your items from there". She once again pointed to the original corner.

Mildred checked the goods, pastries and bread mainly. "They're all here", said Mildred in a surprised manner.

"Aye, Jimmy had your order sent over in advance. Said he wants to help you speed your day up. For an extra pastry for your family, and no trouble of course", Mrs. Baker said, with a shake of her head.

Mildred struggled to a smile, and then said, "That's very good of him Mrs. Baker, but I've no need of an extra pastry. Thank you all the same".

"That's as might be, but, I'll have to ask you to sign my ledger before you leave today, if you'll be so kind", said Mrs. Baker.

As Mildred began to advance towards the ledger, which suddenly appeared on the counter and seemed to fall open onto the correct page, Mrs. Baker continued, "Maybe you can call in on Jimmy's wife, and gift her the pastry. For all our sakes, before trouble befalls someone nice".

Mrs. Baker smiled at this and looked wistfully at the ceiling.

"Thank you. I'll consider that", said Mildred.

"That's nice dear. You can call in, when you've finished your round, and tell me your decision", said Mrs. Baker, handing her quill to Mildred.

Mildred smiled. Signed the ledger, and said, "I must be on my way. I will call in if I have time", turned, and began to leave.

"You make sure you do, or tomorrow I might fall asleep with the door locked. Do you hear me?", barked Mrs. Baker.

Mildred opened the door, to the tinkling bell, goods in her basket, and as she waved, she said, "If I have time", and closed the door behind her.

Mrs. Baker grimaced and shook her head from side to side.

Mildred sped down the road. Walking as fast as she could. 'What had she said during the birth of Jimmy's last born? Were there any promises, asked for or given? And why now, is she being asked to resolve a family dispute?', thought Mildred.

Mrs. Baker sighed, and retired to her back room, after replacing her ledger under the counter, and then went to her cupboard to retrieve her crystal ball.

Ethel sat on her bed, facing east, with her Tarot cards laid out before her. 'Can you tell me a story? How was it when you were young?', she thought to the ghostly caller.

Alice sat in the room below, gazing out of the window at Turner's hill. Once again she had seen the stranger, in an unusual uniform go past her window. 'He resembled Graeme slightly, but he was wearing a hat', she thought.

Graeme had finished his morning post delivery, and was returning to his home, from the farm.

Eric looked out of his office window. Far off, he thought he could hear Master Guild laughing. He looked into the yard below, only to see Jimmy ordering Sam around. He could hear the typists typing. Hear occasional calls, yelps and cheers, from the work floor of the mill.

'Is everything going to plan?', he thought he heard the Lord call out.

'Yes, my Lord, just as you requested', he thought back, then added, 'But the last manager .....?'.

'Never mind about that. That is a police matter now. Keep up the good work', he thought he heard the Lord call out.

'Yes my Lord', thought Eric, who then moved from the window, as one of the typists brought some post in.

"These are for you to look at, Mr. Marshall", said the young typist.

"Thank you. Just leave them on the desk, and close the door on your way out", said Eric.

Mildred passed Tuner`s pond and laughed, as she thought, 'One loaf to be left at the Welsh`s, Graeme would be out until close to lunchtime, and that makes the next stop the Knight`s'. With this she smiled.

The end